Palace Intrigue

AURELIA BEAMED WITH ANTICIPATION AND GRACED
Robert with a smile.

At that moment he knew he was in trouble.

"Yes, tomorrow night is Carnival, the Night of the Masks.
We're old enough to go out in disguise now," Aurelia said. "You
must wait for me before you go." She frowned. "It's no fun
alone."

A trace of sadness in her voice made Robert promise despite
misgivings. "All right, it's not like I can refuse the order of the
princess."

Her voice fried him to ash. "It's not an order, Robert, but even
if it was, I expect my friends to have enough courage to refuse
an invitation."

Nothing had lengthened her temper over the last four years.
He resorted to humor, the only defense availab' ⸍ swept her
a mocking bow. "I'll be your lifelong friend' won't
put up with being pushed around."

"Really?" Her eyes danced. She spl ₊t his
chest and pushed, hard.

Robert held his footing w ᵣ. "Yes, and
thank you for the invitation. waist with his
hands and twirled her toward her ₊ ₊aiting friends. His
mind spun as he looked down at her la ₊ ₊ng face. He could not
imagine why someone was trying to kill her.

Other Books You May Enjoy

For Mom and Dad—
without whom nothing would ever have been written.

And for Shandi—
who will write her own one day.

Contents

Aurelia

Prologue

DEATH DISTURBED THE NIGHT. THE SOUND OF squeaking wheels grew louder, as did the clicking of horse hooves scraping across cobblestones. A rickety old wagon, its simple board bed held together with rusty screws, pulled up against the back of the palace.

Two servants slipped from the shadows, a bearded footman and a wiry kitchen maid with a shuttered lantern in her hand. The footman put his back and shoulder strength into opening an old storage-room door. It had not been moved for some time. Finally, the harsh brush of sliding splinters overcame the friction. A loud squeak echoed into the stillness as he pulled his hands away from the door, satisfied the gap was wide enough.

Meanwhile the maid had rushed toward the driver in the wagon seat and gestured for him to follow her inside. A scraggly, aged man climbed down from his perch, one mud-crusted boot at a time sliding into its foothold and landing less than gracefully upon the ground. The woman tried to encourage him to hurry but received only a sullen grumbling about arthritis on a cold night.

Her face tight with worry, she led both men through the doorway, passing shelves of flour, sugar, and other baking ingredients on her way toward the abandoned cellar. At the top of the staircase, she lifted the lantern shutter to reveal a burning candle, and the group began a descent into the darkness, keeping their hands on the jittery, loose banister.

They hovered above a bulky lump draped in a linen sheet at the bottom of the stairway. Words were exchanged in rasping whispers, though no one was nearby to overhear the conversation. The footman's face dripped with sweat, and the woman's hands trembled, causing the lantern to shake and the light to flicker along empty walls.

In contrast to the nervous servants, the driver simply went about his job as he did every night. He asked the necessary questions, frowned at the distance he was told to travel, and nodded as his payment was increased.

Then the three lifted the awkward object, still wrapped within its sheet, and packed it up the stairs and out of the palace, where they loaded it onto the back of the wagon. Though the wagon bed had been empty, a lingering stench of decay caused the maid to pale and move away in fear of growing nauseous.

The footman dug his hand into a pocket and pulled out a thin purse of money to place in the older man's callused palm. Having received payment, the driver nodded, slipping the purse into a pocket under his frayed, black coat. He pulled up the wagon flap and slid the latch into place. Then, at the same slow pace with which he had climbed down, he negotiated his way back up to his original perch. The well-trained horses waited patiently for him to unwind the reins, and a croaked "Giddyap" swung the wagon into motion.

As the wheels rapped their way down the road, the two servants exhaled with the relief of having finished an undesired task. The woman shuddered and said, "I never thought I'd be dealing with the likes of him when I undertook this job."

The footman murmured his agreement, sliding shut the obstinate door. A chill wind picked up, encouraging both servants to hurry along the path. They slipped through a stone doorway and entered the warm interior of a kitchen in the tumultuous midst of serving a royal banquet.

Down the road, no more than half a mile, the tattered driver hunched over the wagon seat in a futile attempt to fend off the cold. His stomach did not turn when he thought of his cargo. Even if he had been aware it was the body of the princess's meal taster, the knowledge would have mattered little to him beyond its contribution to the purse in his pocket. To him, the body was just another corpse, resting on cracked boards as the wagon lurched its way toward an unmarked mass grave.

Chapter One
PALACE INTRIGUE

ON THE NIGHT OF HER YOUNGER SISTER'S COMING-out party, Aurelia almost died. Of boredom. Her ankle itched as though a single ant were casually creeping over her flesh. She squirmed and stared blankly at the banquet-hall floor. If only she had not worn the violet silk with the stiff lace ruffle on the bottom. She longed to reach down and scratch, but years of royal training had not been entirely lost. She could not afford such a dramatic movement while her father was speaking.

The king stood at the head of the banquet table, his pale eyes staring at the guests' foreheads. His gold crown flattened his prematurely gray hair beneath its weight, and only his slate-gray mustache moved as he droned, "Loyalty and respect are the highest attributes of a young woman." *Please.* Aurelia raised her eyes to the fresco on the ceiling.

The back of her gilt chair bit into her shoulder blades, and the heat generated by close bodies made the dab of face paint on her cheeks gleam. Her lady's maid had dared her to wear the paint, and Aurelia had never refused a dare in her seventeen years.

Thinking was becoming a trial in this stifling atmosphere. Must nearly every lord and lady in the kingdom attend Melony's coming-out party? Where was the appeal in seeing Aurelia's younger sister dance with every titled man in the room? And why must all the dull society members insist upon participating in the celebration?

Aurelia reached toward her dessert plate and crushed the remaining cake crumbs beneath her fork. The rich smell of chocolate clashed with the multitude of perfumes oozing off the guests. Brocade sleeves and frock coats rustled as the speech dragged on, and the whalebone stays in Aurelia's corset dug into her diaphragm. *Breathe,* she told herself. *It's going to be a long night, but then it will finally be over.*

For weeks the entire staff had hurtled back and forth, preparing for Melony's debut. The ballroom and banquet-hall floors were waxed, and tall crimson candles in golden candelabras lit up every corner of the rooms. Long-stemmed roses sprang forth in bouquets of fifteen, one for each of the fifteen years leading up to this exceptional birthday. The pale green silk for Melony's dress had been imported a year in advance, and the palace musicians had been practicing just as long. At first Aurelia had enjoyed the beautiful dance rhythms haunting the palace hallways, but she had long since come to associate the sound of tuning up with the grinding of an oncoming headache.

At least her sister was enjoying herself. Sitting on Aurelia's right, in sharp contrast to her older sister's dark features and darker mood, Melony glowed. Her blond hair glistened in the candlelight and her green eyes matched the sparkle of the emerald necklace at her throat. A smile of sheer pleasure spread across her face. Any other observer might have assumed the brilliant smile was for the king, but Aurelia noted her sister's darting glances toward the end of the long table. Which young noble had captured Melony's interest this time?

Aurelia leaned over to whisper the question in her sister's ear, but a sudden wave of champagne glasses interrupted. "To Tyralt," the king said, his voice gaining in strength, "the most powerful kingdom on the southern coast."

Noting the hesitation on the faces of several of the foreign guests, Aurelia took a sip of champagne. She doubted her father's tactless statement was an accident. He preferred to use words rather than armies to maintain Tyralt's legacy of power within the region.

"I am told we live in an Age of Reason," the king continued, "of Rationality, of Enlightenment." His face cracked a smile as he aimed his glass in Melony's direction. "But I ask you, gentlemen, of what use is reason in the face of beauty?"

A round of chuckles rippled along the table, cleansing the air of the earlier tension. "To Melony, a true jewel of the realm," the king said.

"To Melony," the guests echoed with enthusiasm.

The gold clock chimed ten. At last! Time for the dancing to begin. The king stepped forward, offered his arm to his younger daughter, and led Melony out through the wide archway connecting the banquet hall to the ballroom.

As the crowd's eager eyes focused on the pair positioning themselves for the opening waltz, Aurelia knew her chance had come. Quickly she reached up to secure her tiara. Then, bending down, skirt hitched up, she scratched her ankle in a highly satisfying, undignified manner.

Now for the agony of the ballroom.

Aurelia lifted her empty glass and twirled its thin stem between her fingers, stalling until the final strains of the waltz came to an end. She admired her sister's powers of persuasion. The king had opposed the playing of modern waltz music among the usual minuets and gavottes. He feared the close waltz hold would invite scandal, but Melony had pleaded with her innocent eyes and won the day.

Now the king's gaze lifted from Melony's face and reeled Aurelia in. Duty called. She set down the glass, stood up, and stepped into the rapidly filling ballroom.

A towering gray wig promptly blocked her view. "Oh, my dear, you have grown up," gushed the female owner of the powdered wig. "You were a little sprig of a girl in your father's wedding train the last time I saw you."

Aurelia peered at the petite, older woman, identifying her as a duchess from several kingdoms over. "You must be mistaking me for my sister Melony. I was not present at my father's second wedding."

"Perhaps not at the actual ceremony, but you were a member of the original wedding train." The duchess placed a gloved hand above her mouth as if sharing a secret. "I remember the rehearsal. You had a tantrum because you disliked the frilly dress, and you tore the bows and ruffles right off. Your father removed you from the wedding because your stepmother was so upset. My, how you have changed."

Not as much as you think. Aurelia eyed the woman's ridiculous wig and overblown skirt with hidden distaste. Thanks to the queen's desire to display her natural assets, the tall wigs, bulky panniers, and wide hoops that were still the rage in neighboring kingdoms had disappeared from Tyralian court fashion. Foreign guests such as this woman were easy to identify. Even the foreign men in their plumed hats and buckled shoes stood out next to the bare heads and plain boots of native Tyralians.

"Of course your stepsister took over your role in the actual wedding. She did a lovely job for a three-year-old. One would have thought she was born royal."

Aurelia put on a weak smile. "Melony was two at the time. She had not yet turned three, and you need not refer to her as my stepsister. She is my true sister in all the ways which matter."

"Yes, I'm not surprised you feel that way. It was so good of your father to adopt the child when he married her mother. Such a blessing both Melony and the queen have been to the entire kingdom."

Aurelia stepped aside in a discreet attempt to withdraw, but the duchess dropped her voice and continued. "And such a shame about your brother's death and your mother's disappearance. Prior to the announcement about the new wedding, there was a great deal of concern. People feared your father might never recover from his grief." She opened her fan. "The rumors! I remember my aunt telling me her husband told her the king of Tyralt had locked himself in his library and refused to come out for months. You were too young to remember any of this, I'm sure."

But Aurelia did remember. She remembered the lowering of her brother's coffin and the subsequent pain on her father's face when he announced that her mother had abandoned him and Aurelia. She remembered the hardwood surface of the closed library door. Only a stranger would dredge up those memories in this reckless fashion. "I am sorry, but I must—"

The woman barreled on, plunging into even more personal territory. "Well, my dear, when are you going to find yourself a husband?"

A drunken lord in a white cravat chose that moment to join in the conversation. "Yes, Yer Highness. I say ya oughta stop leadin' all the gennlemen on." He squinted red eyes at Aurelia and reached out a pawing hand toward her bodice.

She backed away. Why did perfect strangers insist on making judgments and personal comments?

A serving maid came to the rescue, toppling the contents of her tray all over both the lord and the duchess. The man and woman gaped in alarm at their wine-stained clothing. "Oh, I am sorry!" gasped the maid, then covered her mouth with her hand and gave a discreet nod toward the center of the dance floor.

Recognizing the girl as one of Melony's servants, Aurelia looked up to catch a conspiratorial wink from her sister. The younger princess released a brilliant smile in her direction, then turned to bestow it upon an eager swarm of young swains.

Aurelia grabbed the opportunity to sweep away from the duchess and the lord.

Right into her father's waiting glare. "What has kept you?" He came forward.

"The duchess wished to speak with me. I did not want to offend a guest."

Her father spared a glance for the man and woman dripping in red wine. "You appear to have failed," he said, then turned toward a group of men gathered a few feet behind him. "The duchess is of little import in comparison with the suitors waiting to meet you."

Suitors, my eye! Aurelia noted the gray beards on two of the wealthy nobles coming toward her. Sweat formed inside her long white gloves, and her chest tightened. The music changed to a gavotte, and a hand touched her elbow. She lifted her gaze reluctantly to accept her first offer to dance for the evening.

Robert Vantauge leaned comfortably back against the ballroom wall, his arms linked across his chest, a jaunty tilt to his head. He had been gone from the capital for four years, his father having chosen to move the family to the unsettled northern region of the kingdom. Robert was back under the guise of visiting his cousin Chris. However, Chris, who was standing beside him, had barely received a moment's worth of attention this night.

Robert's eyes followed Aurelia's dancing figure across the room without blinking. They shone very blue under his dark features and wavy brown hair. Many of the nearby girls had observed those eyes but had given up on drawing their gaze.

He was in a state of shock. The scraggly girl he remembered from his childhood had transformed into a young woman: slender, sharp, and stubborn. He could visualize her entrance into the banquet hall earlier that evening. She had walked with confidence, her thick brown hair swept up in an elaborate coif; her diamond tiara dipping down above the dark crescents of her eyebrows; her cinnamon skin gliding over matching cheekbones, raised chin, and the smooth curve of her jawline. She had held her bare shoulders with poise above the neckline of her expensive gown.

He had scarcely recognized her and might not have known

her at all if it were not for those familiar dark eyes, shining with intensity. Upon first glance, he had feared a polished persona had replaced the opinionated rebel from his past, but not much time went by before the polish began to fade. She had fidgeted all through the king's speech, and now she was dissecting the head of some nobleman who had stepped on her foot. Robert grinned in enjoyment at the improper display.

"Well, I pity the crown princess." A female voice slipped under the harmonic music, catching Robert's attention. Aurelia's lady's maid, Daria, stood at his left elbow speaking to Chris. She wore the white gown of servitude, and her typically pale face glowed with a rosy hue against the fabric. Her first full day of married life must have agreed with her, despite the fact that her new husband, being a courier, had not been invited to the party.

Robert joined the conversation. "It's her partner you should take pity on." He nodded toward Aurelia's enraged face as it disappeared in and out behind the colorful screen of spinning couples.

Daria's dark curls swished as she laughed. "Yes, she is giving him the back side of her tongue, which he no doubt deserves. I still pity her. The poor girl is trapped like carrion among the men in this ballroom. Are you aware, Robert, she's already had to refuse seven proposals of marriage?"

"And who forced her to refuse them?" scoffed Chris, pausing in the aimless pursuit of buttoning and unbuttoning his wide sleeve cuffs. A smirk spread across the fine bones of his smooth face, and he lounged against the tall back of a chair with relaxed grace.

Daria shoved him. "You know five of those so-called suitors were old enough to be her father, even her grandfather."

"And what was wrong with the other two?" Robert asked.

"Besides the fact they were only after her money and her title?" Daria bristled. "One was an utter fool. He couldn't even stand up to his father, much less help run a country. The other was cruel." She shuddered. "He beat his own horse."

Robert grimaced. He held animals in higher esteem than most people.

"Now," Daria said, "Aurelia can only wait, knowing sooner or later her father is going to select some suitor and give her no choice but to marry him."

Chris shook his head. "Do you really think Aurelia's that easily overpowered? When has she ever obeyed an order?"

Robert had to agree with his cousin. The Aurelia he remembered had broken as many rules as she had followed. She had talked her way out of more punishments than anyone Robert knew—except for Chris.

"Don't be so certain." Daria's expression grew serious. "Ever since her brother's death, her father has held the kingdom over her head like a giant scepter he can smash her with. If she refuses to marry, she cannot inherit."

"She would lose the kingdom." Robert frowned. "And we would lose a strong leader."

"Her second cousin, the king of Montaine, would take over Tyralt," Chris muttered.

"At least Melony can't inherit." Daria motioned toward the grand portrait of Aurelia's sister hanging on the wall. The younger princess held no claim on the crown through blood. "Can you imagine *her* dealing with a crisis?"

Chris jostled his friend. "Come on, Dar, Melony's not that bad. She's just not Aurelia."

On this point, Robert was not certain he agreed with his cousin. He had never known the younger princess well, but he had observed her telling one person one thing and another the opposite in order to keep both happy. He did not like the idea of being unable to trust the person making decisions for the entire kingdom. His father and mother had taught him to value people who were willing to disagree with him. "Far better that, than to place your trust in someone who will deny you their support in a dangerous situation," his mother had said. One thing Aurelia had never been afraid to do was argue with him, or anyone else for that matter.

"If Aurelia did love someone," Daria continued, ignoring Chris's comment, "she'd probably run away and marry him whether or not her father approved. As it is, she doesn't care a bit for any of those suitors, and she wouldn't gain anything by infuriating the king." Neither Robert nor Chris disagreed. "By refusing to marry, she would just succeed in losing what is most precious to her."

"At the moment," Robert said, nodding toward the princess, "I think she's holding her privacy most precious because she hasn't had any all evening."

Daria smiled, a gleam in her black eyes. "Neither has she had a moment away from those titled aristocrats. I dare you, Robert, to go rescue her."

"And just how would I do that?" he asked.

"Go ask her to dance, of course. Then waltz her this way and out from under her father's watchful eye."

"Don't." Chris gripped Robert's elbow. "Every man who speaks to her these days is put on the palace watch list. They intend to pack her wedding trunks within the year. Anyone who is a potential husband is required to speak with her father, and anyone in the way becomes an object of palace scrutiny."

Aware he was ignoring sage advice, Robert shook the hand off his elbow and took a step forward. "Oh, calm yourself," he teased. "She's danced with ten or fifteen men thus far tonight. By the time anyone gets around to worrying about me, I'll be safely back on the frontier. Of course I'll accept Daria's dare. You obviously aren't up to the challenge, and if I don't, Aurelia may suffocate before I get a chance to talk to her."

Somehow he managed to maneuver through the revolving swirls of silks, taffetas, and velvets overflowing the dance floor. He sidestepped several couples just in time to avoid being stamped on by an ill-placed boot or a high-heeled shoe and emerged, feet intact, just behind his old classmate.

Aurelia shook her head at an insistent partner's demand for a second dance and managed to slip loose of clinging arms. She recoiled, fortunately in Robert's direction. Another lurker reached out a hand for her elbow, but the would-be partner was too late. Robert had her in his grasp, spinning her around to face him.

"How dare you!" Anger flared, transforming the landscape of her face. Sharp lines and angles replaced the smooth curves of her chin and jaw. Muscles tightened around her cheekbones, and her eyebrows spiked as she tried to tug her right hand out of his grip. Her brown eyes boiled with indignation and, due to a fierce tug, her hair arrangement tumbled halfway down her neck.

"Don't snap," Robert scolded, encircling her waist in waltz position. "You'll draw your father's attention, and we'll never escape."

"My father's attention?" The scornful tone let Robert know she had kept the same opinion on this point. She managed to free herself from the dance hold but not the tight grip on her right hand.

Robert tugged her back, whispering, "You are still a falcon, one camouflaged in silk, face paint, and hairpins, but a falcon nonetheless." He waited to see if the old name-calling would stop her from taking flight.

Emotions flicked across her face, first wariness, then surprise, and finally, recognition.

"Robert Vantauge!" Her eyes lit up. "When did you arrive? I thought you had gone off to become a frontier hero and live on the land. You were going to come back with a pack full of furs and stories about how you'd collected them." She eyed the proper attire he had borrowed from Chris, clicking her tongue. "I must say that as a frontiersman, you are an abysmal disappointment. Where are the scars, the hunting knife, and the buckskin jacket?" She could always parry with her tongue as well as he could with a sword.

"I'm afraid I collected more bruises than scars. My knife is in my saddlebags, and my jacket is hanging behind the door in Chris's room. I came for a visit and had the misfortune to arrive last night, too late to attend Daria's wedding and too early to avoid this exercise in elitism."

Aurelia's face darkened.

"And," he added, putting on a forcefully cheerful voice, "just in time to rescue ye fair maid. I have been sent on this mission, risking your wrath, to lead you over to yon comrades." He wagged his head. "'Tis a shame. You seem to have left them yearning for your presence far too long."

Aurelia leaped up to see her friends beyond the crowd of heads.

"No, no, no!" Robert embraced her in waltz position. "We don't want to draw unnecessary attention."

She beamed with anticipation and graced him with a smile.

At that moment he knew he was in trouble.

"You've been bad," she said, "arriving at the palace last night and not bothering to let me know you were here."

"I won't beg your pardon." He grinned. "I was exhausted by the time I arrived. Even Chris barely received three words from me, 'Hello. Good night.' Then today the palace was so hectic I couldn't have grabbed a minute of your time if I was holding your lady's maid at sword point."

"Ha!" She shook her head, knocking off several tenuously placed hairpins. "I will only forgive you if you promise to wait for me tomorrow night before you and Chris leave."

"Tomorrow night?" Her teasing threat was too far out of context for him to manage a smart response.

She laughed at his confusion. "Yes, it's Carnival, the Night of the Masks. Remember all those nasty tricks we used to play on our instructors, like the time we spent the whole night painting the classroom black?"

Robert did remember that night with the paint. He and his friends had been caught, eventually. His father had taken two months to uncover the names of every student involved. Being the daughter of the king was no caramel apple, but being the son of the king's royal spy had its drawbacks as well. Robert had paid for that practical joke long after many of his fellow students had forgotten it had ever occurred.

"We're old enough to go out in disguise now," Aurelia said. "You must wait for me before you go." She frowned. "It's no fun alone."

A trace of sadness in her voice made Robert promise despite misgivings. "All right, it's not like I can refuse the order of the princess."

Her voice fried him to ash. "It's not an order, Robert, but even if it was, I expect my friends to have enough courage to refuse an invitation."

Nothing had lengthened her temper over the last four years. He resorted to humor, the only defense available, and swept her a mocking bow. "I'll be your lifelong friend then, since I won't put up with being pushed around."

"Really?" Her eyes danced. She splayed her hands against his chest and pushed, hard.

Robert held his footing without giving ground. "Yes, and thank you for the invitation." He encircled her waist with his hands and twirled her toward her anxiously waiting friends. His mind spun as he looked down at her laughing face. He could not imagine why someone was trying to kill her.

Chapter Two

PROTEST

"...TOO DANGEROUS."

"...is aware of the danger."

Fragments of voices, restrained in volume but not intensity, filtered through the goose-feather quilt and cotton blankets. Robert burrowed deeper into his sanctuary, thankful the voices were on the other side of the closed door.

The sound of his own name catapulted him awake. "Robert proved last night that he could gain intimate access to her," Uncle Henry told his son. "That is more than her personal guards have managed to achieve."

"We're not talking about escorting her to a party," Chris argued. "We don't know who we're dealing with, and Robert hasn't even been at court for years."

"He grew up here. He knows the principal players well

enough, and it is to his advantage that whoever is behind the plot may not remember him. Even if they do, it is unlikely his role will be suspected for exactly the reasons you just pointed out."

Robert smiled at the familiar words. He had used the same line of thought with his father.

"You can be his source for current information," Uncle Henry went on. "Tell him what you know about everyone. Answer his questions. Connect the web. He can blend in and investigate where I can't, and you can provide him with the insight he's lacking."

Chris sounded unconvinced. "He's had no training. How will he know what to do?"

"His father was the royal spy for fifteen years. He must have thought Robert would be helpful enough. If we do not use him, we may not find out who we're dealing with until it is too late. We have no choice. There is no time."

"Last night makes that painfully clear," Chris grudgingly agreed.

With his cousin's protests out of the way, Robert swung up into sitting position on the bed. "*What* about last night?" he demanded.

Immediately the door swung open. Chris glared into the room, then flung up his hands in a gesture of surrender. "At least he has the eavesdropping part down."

Uncle Henry stepped through the doorway. The stress of

being the king's adviser had added years to his appearance. Gray hair streamed out around his face in wild strands, and tension lined the leathery skin above his long beard and slightly stooped body.

"There was another assassination attempt last night," he said, directing his words to Robert. "You were right about what you told me yesterday. I wrote your father because I need a secret investigator. If he cannot be here, we need you to spy for us. Spend time with Aurelia, and listen for anything suspicious. We must uncover this plot soon. Her life is in grievous danger."

"Has she been hurt?" Robert's thoughts whirled, the real reason for his return to the palace flashing into reality.

"She does not even know about the danger." Chris brushed aside the question, kicking a broken scabbard into a corner beside his collection of loop-hilt smallswords.

Uncle Henry frowned at the scabbard. "You might want to pick that up, Christopher, now that your cousin is in need of our hospitality."

"The maid will get it."

Robert propped the broken scabbard up against the wall. He had been away from the palace too long to feel comfortable taking advantage of the palace staff, but he knew better than to argue with his cousin. Chris had looked far from comfortable sleeping on the sitting-room settee last night, and Robert had no desire to take sides between his cousin and his uncle.

"I must leave," Uncle Henry said, turning to his son. "The

king requires my presence for a public statement this morning, and I need to inform him of my decision to hire Robert on his behalf. Provide your cousin with the details."

As his uncle departed, Robert scrambled from the bed and reached into his saddlebags for a pair of wool trousers.

"You don't want to attract attention by wearing those frontier clothes," said Chris, pulling a pair of breeches from a drawer and tossing them to his cousin. "You can borrow mine while you're here."

Reluctantly, Robert set aside the durable wool. "Tell me about the assassination attempt."

"Dress yourself," Chris replied, plucking a dull practice sword from a hook on the wall, "and let's have this conversation in the practice yard."

"Is that a challenge?"

"If you are going to invade my room for a prolonged period, I at least deserve the pleasure of embarrassing you in combat."

Within minutes, both young men pounded down a servants' stairway. For every formal route in the huge T-shaped palace, another hall or stair allowed servants to negotiate the three floors of the old square structure at the back and the modern east and west wings at the front. The servants' routes, being the most direct paths anywhere, were Chris's and Robert's preferred mode of travel. Dim stone walls flashed by, and Robert felt his chest tighten. Narrow spaces made him nervous.

He burst out the door into the practice yard. Fresh air

cleansed his lungs as his cousin tugged him onto the flat, sanded surface. The palace's stone walls and sculpted windows stretched up on two sides, and the guardhouse bordered the yard's southern edge. A handful of men crossed swords near the guardhouse wall, though most had apparently abandoned the pursuit earlier in the day. Chris led the way toward the center of the yard, far enough away from the other men to avoid being overheard. "On guard," he said.

Robert complied. "Well, what happened last night?" he demanded.

Chris's sword leaped into action. "Aurelia's meal taster died of poison."

"Poison?" Robert blocked his cousin's thrust.

"Yes." Chris shifted position. "It was in the banquet cake, only the slice set aside for the crown princess. The assassin used too much, though. Otherwise the meal taster wouldn't have shown signs of illness until after the cake reached the table."

"Who could have had access to the cake after it was sliced and before the meal taster took a bite?"

"The person who can answer that question is dead."

Robert blocked another swing in frustration. The long trip and late night had taken more out of him than he had realized. He should not be sweating this early in a practice. "The first attempt involved poison as well. Have the guards spoken with the apothecaries in the city?"

"They did. Any apothecary could have mixed the poison.

Regular customers buy it to kill rats. The buyer could have transferred it to the cake without the apothecary's knowledge."

"Did guards track down customers who bought the poison?"

"There were hundreds, and most of the names were not written down." Chris leaped back as a blunt edge grazed his stomach. "Curse it, Rob! When did you find time to practice? I thought sword fighting was considered a frivolous art on the frontier."

"Not by my father. A sword is more accurate than a pistol. Besides, I'm still aiming to defeat you."

"One can always dream."

They circled to the right, assessing each other. Chris's lean body gave no sign of tiring. His feet stepped smoothly over the white sand, and his brown eyes skimmed over his cousin, no doubt noting the telling beads of sweat on Robert's forehead.

"Ah, but I have nothing to lose," Robert argued. "It takes only one win to challenge the reputation of the palace's best swordsman. If I don't win today, there's always tomorrow. I prefer to practice at seven o'clock, though, have it out of the way early."

"Then you can find yourself another partner." Chris feinted left. "I'm not waking up early to endanger my reputation."

Swords clashed and for a moment the conversation stalled. Chris swept his sword in a swift arc, then brought it down with strength.

Robert barely managed to bring his own weapon up in defense. "Two assassination attempts in as many months." He groaned, his arms straining against the pressing weight. "We've got to try something."

"Three."

"What?"

"Three assassination attempts." Chris knocked the sword from Robert's hand. "There was another one last week."

Aurelia watched Robert's sword skid across the sand and stop with a spinning flourish twenty feet in front of her. "He's improved," Daria said, stepping out the doorway onto the marble path that skirted the palace.

"Apparently not enough," Aurelia replied, lifting her gaze to study Robert.

Without noting her presence, he reached a bare hand down to retrieve his weapon. Too intent on his objective, she supposed. Even in traditional black breeches and a loose silk shirt, he did not fit in with the palace surroundings. He wore neither a coat nor gloves and moved with a quick urgency foreign to the fabricated ease of court life. Though he shared the same medium height and slender bone structure as his cousin, Aurelia noted little of Chris's catlike grace or detached attitude. There was too much life in Robert's face.

"Now I know why you chose to come out this door instead of the front," Daria teased, tugging her friend away from the practice yard and around the east wing. This side of the palace bustled with sound. Outdoor servants laughed and chatted as they traipsed out of the extended servants' quarters. Hammers and anvils pounded from the blacksmith's forge and construction sheds, and farther in the distance, calves bawled in the animal barns.

Aurelia walked by most of the outer buildings without a glance, but her eyes dwelt fondly on the welcoming arches of the palace stables, then drifted with longing toward the stone wall surrounding the royal arena. She had no time for riding today. Instead the two girls rounded the northeast corner and hurried across the earthen courtyard on their way to the front gate.

They passed a gatehouse and stopped at the arched opening in the outer wall surrounding the palace. A young man with an oblong face and a thatch of black hair stood under the arch. "Would you like me to summon a carriage, Your Highness?" he asked.

Aurelia frowned at the use of formal address. "How would you like it if I referred to you as Private Micae, Filbert?" she scolded.

A bright red flush stormed the face of Daria's older brother. The lady's maid laughed. "He wouldn't care for it at all, especially as your father promoted him to corporal last week."

If possible, Filbert's red cheeks grew brighter.

"You should have heard our father go on about it," Daria continued. "The son of the head groom, a corporal of the guard! I thought everyone in the palace must know by now."

Aurelia grinned. "Congratulations."

Filbert managed to gain enough control over his tongue to repeat his earlier question. "W-would you like me to summon a carriage?" He avoided using her name.

"We are only traveling to the market," she said. "We can reach there by foot faster than even your father could prepare a carriage. Besides, you know I prefer to walk or ride in the open air. I can see the people and the city that way."

"Very well, Your Highness," Filbert said with a bow.

He was truly hopeless. She could never persuade him to treat her like a common acquaintance.

As the girls brushed past the curling metal sides of the open gateway, four guards came out of the gatehouse and attached themselves in an unwanted train. Aurelia ignored their presence, instead allowing her eyes to caress the view as she walked down Palace Hill toward Tyralt City.

The smooth cobblestone road wound its way down the steep slope to the wide valley at its base. Halfway down, the graceful Tyralt River joined the path, flowed along the curving roadside, then skirted the lower edge of the slope, swept back in serpentine formation around the city center, and drifted east into the gray-green bay. Scattered bridges arched across the river waters, and willow trees draped their leaves and branches over the bank in sheltering parasols.

A handful of white stone buildings with red clay roofs speckled Palace Hill, but at the base, they dominated. The most populated city in Tyralt spread in a sweeping fan, its edges kept in check by the open bay and a thick stone wall. The main road, lined by two rows of planted maples, sliced a direct path from the base of the hill to the gate at the far north end. City streets, many too narrow for even a single carriage, traced intricate patterns through diverse neighborhoods. Tenements crowded the northwest corner between the western gate and the main gate, and a bustling rim of boardinghouses and taverns lined the port and the bay's deep indentation on the city's east side. Merchants' shops and the workplaces of skilled laborers filled the southeast corner, and off to the left stretched the colorful collage of the marketplace.

"Poor Filbert." Daria laughed. "I'm afraid he is as besotted with you as he was when we took class together. I have introduced him to plenty of more appropriate girls, but you know my brother. He sees someone in a gown and he can't pry his tongue off the roof of his mouth."

"Filbert is sweet," Aurelia said. "Maybe I should run off with him and deprive my father of the chore of finding me a husband."

"Don't you dare!" Daria's eyes sparked.

"I thought you were above class distinctions, Dar," Aurelia teased. "Do not tell me your brother is not a fine enough match for me." She wrinkled her nose. "At least he is only a few years older than we are, instead of a few decades like the men my father prefers."

"My brother is fine enough for any woman." Daria straightened. "But you are the last person he should marry. You are too..."

"Too what?" Aurelia knew what her friend meant but wanted to see if Daria would follow through with the statement.

"Too everything. Too headstrong, too changeable, too opinionated. You would be the death of my sweet brother."

"I guess I shall have to give up any hope of becoming your sister, then, if that is the way you feel about me."

Daria smiled, squeezing Aurelia's waist. A white carriage rattled past, its silk curtains tied back, and the stylish woman inside frowned at the lady's maid's presumption. Aurelia lifted her chin and linked arms with her companion. "Thank you for making time for me today."

They moved forward, arm in arm, the expansive marketplace soon enveloping them in shoulder-high pyramids of beets, turnips, and potatoes, anything sturdy enough to have survived the winter and early spring in storage. "I still can't believe you're moving so far away. What am I going to do without you?" Aurelia moaned as she picked up an onion, then ran her hand over the slick surface of the peel.

"I'm sure you'll manage," Daria said, plucking the onion from her friend's hand and returning it to the produce cart. The vendor's face fell as the lady's maid tugged the princess away.

Sounds of life and death permeated the marketplace: the shouts of men in heavy aprons tossing thick trout and slapping them on scales; the pounding of butchers' knives cleaving through bone, muscle, and tissue; the complaints of animals tied up on the outskirts, baying and barking, squawking and squealing.

And through the sounds, the smells: climbing into every corner, every cart, every cloak. The rich scents of ground cinnamon and chili powder, the sickening sweetness of bricked molasses, the dusty aroma of carved oak and pressed cedar. Sage and garlic, petals and powder, feathers and fur.

Daria pulled Aurelia past the food toward the dry goods.

"I'm sure I won't manage," Aurelia said, picking up the conversation where it had left off. "How would I be able to go shopping today without your help? Everyone in the city would recognize my Carnival mask if I couldn't send you to purchase it for me."

Daria dropped her voice, glancing back at the guards behind them. "We both know how you would get around that." She raised her voice. "The truth is you could have had the mask made in the palace if you had bothered to plan ahead."

"Not if I want it to remain a secret. Some of the servants try, but not one of them can resist a good conversation. They would start hinting about the materials, and within half an hour the entire disguise would be common knowledge."

"Still, you needn't have left it until the day I leave."

"Why not? I needed a chance to say good-bye. Besides, I hadn't decided to participate in Carnival until last night."

Daria winked, sliding two fingers along the loose end of her sash. "Convenient of Robert to show up just as I'm leaving, isn't it?"

Aurelia shoved her friend good-naturedly. "It's not the same. He's just visiting."

"Well, I can think of worse classmates to have visit. He's been gone for four years. You ought to have plenty to say to each other. Imagine if your mother hadn't insisted on a school and a quality education for all the palace children. None of us might have become friends."

Aurelia did not want to talk about her mother. If her mother had really cared about children, she would not have left. She would have stayed at the palace long enough to see her daughter grow up.

"I wish your husband didn't work for Lord Lester," Aurelia told her friend. "His estate is halfway to the frontier. The man doesn't even come to court."

"Lucky for me," Daria said as she stepped around a crate. "Lord Lester is notorious for refusing to attend palace events. He's certain to send another scrawled message excusing himself from the next state function. My husband will have to deliver it, and I won't be shy about joining him."

"How often can that happen?" Aurelia ducked under a basket of herbs hanging from a stall canopy.

"Already enough for Thomas and me to meet, fall in love, and marry."

"What if Thomas is promoted from courier?" Aurelia sighed. "Besides, you'll have a new life, new friends, and eventually children. The last thing you'll want is to spend weeks traveling to come visit me."

"Nonsense." Daria brushed away the commonsense statement. "Who wouldn't want to traverse muddy roads, fog-ridden forests, and washed-out crossings for the honor of attending a royal function?"

"Lord Lester."

"Well, perhaps Lord Lester."

Aurelia squeezed her friend in a fierce hug. "I'm not sure I can survive without you."

As they broke apart, Aurelia ran her eyes over the nearby stalls. This section of the market hummed as busily as the one the girls had just left. Vendors shook out woven blankets to display brilliant patterns. Artisans spread out cloth dolls, glass carafes, and embroidered lace. Aurelia's gaze skimmed over fine wood carvings and glazed clay.

A vendor's cart piled high with Carnival items drew her attention. Painted wooden wands spilled out of a deep basket. Leather belts and colored kerchiefs hung from hooks. Beaded capes, skirts, and cloaks draped over the sides, and masks filled the shelves: five rows of them. Faces of genies and gypsies, mice and magicians, frogs and fishermen.

Aurelia froze. "The mask on the cart, second row up."

"Which one?"

"Guess."

Within moments, Daria nodded. "I'll get it. Where am I meeting you?"

Aurelia motioned toward a quadrant of stone walls at the heart of the marketplace. Leaving her friend behind, she set out for the square. All four guards followed her, their braided uniforms and polished scabbards drawing the usual stares.

She paused outside a dressmaker's shop but did not go in. Even the best dressmaker could not accept an order with less than a day to complete it. As soon as Aurelia had spotted her chosen mask, she had mentally selected a dress from the stock of unworn ball gowns and party wear cluttering up her wardrobe. At least some use would come out of the seamstresses' zealous attempts to help her attract a husband.

Her mind still focused on her costume, she stepped into an arched tunnel leading toward the center of the square. The guards suddenly pushed ahead, blocking her path. Caught by surprise, she stared past them at men, women, and children crowding the inner plaza.

A throng of shaking fists, shuffling feet, and shoving elbows filled the space. Eyes flashed. Lips flared. Shouts tumbled over one another like viscious dogs. The crowd's anger grew tangible, swelling and feeding itself, all directed toward the square's centerpiece—a statue of her father.

The guards pulled back as if to leave, but Aurelia refused to withdraw, her eyes glued to the statue's face. Her father gazed back at her, not with the weary look she recognized, but with the pride she imagined he must have worn in her early childhood—before her brother had died and her mother had left. She could not allow that statue to be destroyed.

A barrage of rocks and sticks flew through the air, slamming into the statue. Bodies moved as if to topple it. "Wait!" Aurelia forced her way through the guards. "Talk to me. Tell me why you do this. Tell me what you want."

A hush engulfed the mob as she stepped out from under the arch. Fists fell, shoulders dropped, and mouths closed. People waited in a ring of suspended tension. She walked through that ring, stepping into the square's center and laying her hand in the enlarged carving of her father's own palm. Standing in front of the populace, she could feel the weight of expectations settle on her shoulders—the people's hopes for a better future, their faith in her as a leader, her own dread that she would let them down.

"You, sir," she said to a man in a torn black vest, "why are you here?"

He rubbed a hand across the whiskers on his chin as though trying to decide whether to answer, then said, "I'm a vendor, Your Highness. I run a stall in the market and make just enough coin for my family. I reckon the same is true for most of these folks." Nods scattered the crowd. "But this mornin' the king announced a new tax on every stall and cart in the marketplace."

Why had her father not told her? There had been no mention of a new tax at the last council meeting.

"I wouldn't mind if the money were goin' toward the city or likely to help my family in some way," the vendor said.

"But it isn't!" a woman shouted.

The man continued: "Your father called it a market tax, but it's to pay for state functions. That means more spectacles like that fancy party held last night in your sister's honor. He's already drained the city coffers fixin' up the palace."

"And it's not like any of us will ever be invited to that monstrosity!" added the woman.

"We can't none of us afford to lose our stalls," the vendor said, "but we have a right to say how our money should be spent."

"I'll speak with my father," Aurelia told the crowd. "Perhaps he does not understand how the tax will affect you."

"He *would* know," the man replied, "if we had somebody to speak our piece at the palace. As it is, we can't control our own future."

Understanding flickered through Aurelia's heart. The man had a point, one far stronger than the weight of his own purse. "I'll share your concerns," she said. "You have my word. The people deserve a voice at the palace."

Mumbles of approval rippled through the square. *Good,* she thought, *maybe now they will disband in peace.* A new silence descended, broken only by the rustle of a petticoat as Daria stepped from the crowd and moved to her friend's side in support. Aurelia let out a slow breath.

Then a disturbance bubbled at the back of the crowd. People shifted, grumbling protests. A black cap forged its way forward, ripping a seam through the wave of bodies. Closer and closer it sped. Then a shout.

Harsh steel flared; four swords flashed. Voices raised in rekindled anger. The silence whipped into fury, and strong hands forced Aurelia to the ground.

Chapter Three
CARNIVAL

"WHAT WERE YOU THINKING?" THE QUEEN'S COLD voice cut into Aurelia's heart. Elise did not bother to stand or turn around to speak to her stepdaughter. Instead, icy blue eyes and a frigid stare reflected out of the vanity mirror. Elise's pale neck showed bare below a tight knot of black hair, and her rigid back and shoulders remained frozen and erect against the white backdrop of the vanity table and dressing-room windows. "The guards tell me you almost caused a riot this morning."

"They almost caused the riot," Aurelia protested from the doorway. She wanted to talk to her father. She did not want to defend herself to her stepmother. "If they had not drawn their swords, Daria would have recognized the boy in the crowd, and the conflict would have ended."

"What boy?" The queen picked up a jewelry box with a heart etched on the lid.

"He was just a boy wearing a black cap. Daria paid his father too much for an item she purchased in the market, and the boy's father sent his son to return the money. The man needn't have bothered, but it was the honorable thing to do. Except the boy got caught behind the crowd; and when it quieted, he tried to come forward to give Daria the money."

"Thank heavens that girl has finally gone off with her new husband. I hope you select a more suitable lady's maid to replace her."

Aurelia's temper flared. She had missed her friend's departure because of her stepmother's summons. "Daria isn't to blame. If the guards had waited, the boy would have explained himself, and there wouldn't have been a problem; but they drew their swords and set off the entire crowd. The guards are the ones who ought to be reprimanded."

"You're lucky more guards arrived when they did." Elise arched her sharp eyebrows. "Or the episode could have been disastrous, not only for you, but for your father."

"Let me see him. If what the protesters said was true, they had a good argument. Father should hear about it."

"The city rabble cause enough problems without you helping them. They can't be expected to understand politics. But you, Aurelia, should have known better. Your father does not have time to discuss this with you right now. He is preparing for

an important guest. You may speak with him at the next council meeting." The queen removed an icicle necklace from the
box. "In the meantime, you should remain within the palace."

"But tonight is Carnival!"

"Which you won't be attending." Elise snapped the box shut.

You certainly won't stop me. Aurelia whirled and stalked from
the room.

Ornate tapestries and gold filigree taunted her as she moved
down the hallway. It angered her to think the queen's expensive
taste had damaged her father's reputation in the city. The glossy
furniture, walls of embroidered cloth, and paintings on the ceilings all reflected Elise's own extravagance.

At times Aurelia wished her father had never met Elise. But
that was not entirely fair. If Aurelia's own mother had never
left, he would not have had to remarry. And then his daughter
would never have had to walk the gauntlet of her stepmother's
disdain. Besides, Elise could not be blamed for failing to love a
child whose own mother had abandoned her.

At least with the king's second marriage, Aurelia had gained
a sister.

A hush fell on the princesses' shared parlor as Aurelia entered
the room. The bevy of Melony's lady's maids rose as one from
their seats and exited until only the two sisters remained.

"Palace gossip must have traveled fast." Aurelia hurled herself
onto the settee. "Honestly, Mel, sometimes I think you should
be the crown princess."

Her sister gave a soft laugh and twisted a jade bracelet on her wrist. "Without a hint of royal blood in my veins? I suspect your cousin Montaine might disagree."

Aurelia groaned. "He'd probably swoop down and bury us all in war before the month was out."

"And he would win. The other kingdoms would never support a disruption undermining the line of inheritance."

"I know." Aurelia lifted a silk pillow and squeezed it to her chest. "And the truth is, I love my kingdom but you're the one with the gift for court life."

"Yes, well." Melony sank down beside her. "Our father is rather fond of tradition."

Aurelia gave a weak smile, then threaded her fingers through her sister's hand. "You're the only person who understands the pressure of being his daughter."

Melony tapped the edge of the settee, then hopped up. "There are some advantages," she declared, swinging open the door to her sitting room. "Come out, girls!"

The flood of lady's maids swept back into the parlor. Two girls rushed to the bench at the pianoforte. Another four returned to a game board, and three crowded onto the window seat. The youngest girl, no more than eleven years old, hid behind her mistress's flowing skirts.

Anticipation shone on Melony's unblemished face as she looked at her older sister. "I know you lost Daria this morning, and I thought you might like to select one of my lady's maids as your new personal attendant."

Aurelia's jaw dropped. *As if I could replace Daria that easily.*

Her sister seemed to read her expression and reached out to embrace her. "I know you had a terrible day today, and I want to help. Half the girls are technically assigned to you anyway."

Of course Melony meant well.

Aurelia wrinkled her forehead. "I prefer a smaller entourage. I can't imagine how you keep them all busy."

"Oh, they go on missions for me." Melony twirled around. "They inform the chef of my preferences for the day and check on the status of my new gowns." She dropped her voice. "They turn in papers to my instructors and invent excuses for me to avoid class. Most of the time, though," she whispered in Aurelia's ear, "they carry messages back and forth to young men."

Aurelia groaned. She had no desire to command a unit of giggling adolescents. Instead, she focused on the child who had been hiding behind her sister's skirts. Wide hazel eyes overwhelmed the pale face. A spattering of pink freckles sprinkled the sharp cheekbones, and a fringe of mousy brown hair frizzed loose from its shell comb. *If I have to lose my best friend, I might as well select a lady's maid I can intimidate into leaving me alone.* "What is your name?" Aurelia asked, squatting down to the child's level.

"Min-Minuet."

"Do you think you could come assist me, Minuet?"

The girl's big eyes grew even wider, and for a moment Aurelia thought the child might run away. "Y-y-yes, Your Highness."

"Wonderful." Aurelia glanced up to see her sister's delighted reaction, then returned her attention to the lady's maid. "I'm in for the evening," she lied, not wanting to involve Minuet in her rebellious Carnival plans. "So I won't require your help until morning. If you would like to remain here in the meantime, you are welcome to do so."

"Th-thank you, Your Highness."

Unencumbered, Aurelia slipped out of the parlor and hurried through her personal sitting room into her bedchamber. She grinned in the mirror as she tugged out painful hairpins. Time to dress for the night's adventure. Soft waves fell past her shoulders. Brown hair, brown eyes, brown skin. Nothing worth taking note of next to her sister's stunning looks; but tonight, at least, that did not matter.

Removing bodice and skirt, Aurelia ducked her head into the depths of her closet. Her fingertips, rather than her eyes, recognized the feathery material, and she pulled the dress from the darkness. Soft fabric flowed out into the light. Blackish brown bars speckled a white background.

Aurelia lifted the dress over her head and slid her arms through the narrow straps. The skirt fluttered down over her petticoat, and the bodice settled into place. She buttoned the front from the waist to the low neckline and tied the slender cord around her middle. Leaving her throat bare, she slipped her feet into gold slippers with hard soles, then brushed out her tangled hair until it lay smooth. She covered her gown with a dark blue cloak and tugged open the bureau's bottom drawer.

The mask lay threateningly inside, begging her to put it on in defiance of her stepmother's order. *I'm going out tonight and this disguise is going to allow me to swoop right out the front gate.* Aurelia scooped up the mask and gazed at it for a moment before hiding it under the folds of her cloak. At least one other person would appreciate her choice.

Robert laughed at his cousin's costume.

Chris sat perched on the sitting-room stool not ten feet away, his legs curled around the stool legs, his eyes locked on the door to the hall. The intensity on his face and the awkward position itself were funny, but Chris's costume made the entire scene ridiculous. White feathers covered his tunic, and a draping fan of red, white, and green feathers sprouted below his lower back. He wore tight white trousers above stockings stuffed in orange boots, and his rooster mask with its three-inch red comb hung below his neck.

"Can you crow?" Robert teased.

"Cockadoodledoo!" His cousin scooped up a velvet cushion from Uncle Henry's rattan chair and flung it.

The velvet object spiraled through the air. Robert ducked. It bounced off the settee on which he was sitting, skimmed over the cherrywood stand, and slowed to a halt beside a porcelain vase on top of a table. The vessel rocked back and forth on the veneered surface before settling into place.

Eyeing the vase, Chris suggested, "Let's go over the second assassination attempt."

Robert's face sobered. "Did it involve poison as well?"

"No, a saddle. Aurelia had to cancel a ride at the last minute. She left her saddle on her mare, and one of the grooms took the horse out for exercise. A strap ripped right along the seam. The groom came off in the middle of a run and broke his collarbone. According to Daria's father, the saddle must have been tampered with."

"The groom was riding sidesaddle?"

"Aurelia only rides sidesaddle under duress." Chris chuckled. "It was a regular saddle."

"May I see it?"

Chris ran a thumb over the edge of a feather on his shirt. "You may if you can look at it without drawing Aurelia's attention."

"She still has it?"

"The servants couldn't take it from her without explaining what went wrong. Instead, they had it repaired and hung it back up as if it had never been damaged."

Discomfort crawled along Robert's shoulders. How could he keep Aurelia safe if she remained unaware of the danger? He stood up, paced to the back of the room, and turned around. "They should tell her what's going on."

"They can't." Chris hopped off his stool. "And neither can you. The king is adamant about that. He doesn't want his daughter frightened. That's why Uncle Henry arranged for an undertaker to secretly pick up the body of the meal taster last night. The king did not want Aurelia asking questions."

Robert's head swam. "How am I going to stay close to her if I can't tell her why I'm here?"

"You're not her bodyguard. You can't protect her that way. You have to be free to investigate."

Robert shuddered. His father's voice echoed in his mind. *You have to start with the victim. The key lies there if you can—*

Knocking interrupted the thought. Chris lunged for the latch, and Aurelia stepped in, closing the door behind her.

She slipped off her cloak and put on her mask. Dark eyes shone within gold circles, each ring surrounded by an almond-shaped outline of deeper gold. White feathers arched back over her hairline, and a hooked beak curved from the bridge of her nose down to a fine tip just over the rounded base of her chin. The top of the beak glistened gold as well, then blended into shimmering silver.

Robert's face crinkled with approval. "A falcon," he said. "I always told you the nickname fit."

"And why is that?" she asked.

"Because you tend to attack an opponent with swiftness and ferocity." He swept her a comic bow, then stepped closer, running his gaze over her entire outfit. She stood nearly as tall as he did, the top of her mask reaching his forehead. "My lady," he said, taking her hand in his white-gloved one, "clearly we shall have to work hard to remain your escorts this night."

Aurelia scrutinized her companions' costumes. "I can see Chris is a rooster, complete with a comb and feathers I'm sure he plans to show off this evening." She earned a wink. "But what are you?" She eyed Robert's white cravat and black frock coat with distaste. "Surely you don't intend to masquerade as a gentleman?"

Chris smirked, and Robert held up a hand to ward off the accusation. "Ah, but you have not yet seen my entire costume." He retreated to his cousin's room, where he grabbed a mask and a pack of cards on a string. The man's face in the mask grinned up at him with a curling black mustache. Robert slipped the face over his head and returned to the sitting room.

"A gambler!" Aurelia proclaimed, snapping her fingers in approval.

"Not just a gambler." Chris flipped over the cards in Robert's hand to display them faceup. "If you look closely, you will notice he has stacked the deck."

"Yes, my dishonesty astounds me." Robert hung the cards around his neck.

Aurelia slipped back under her cloak, and her companions did likewise with their own. "Your cheating doesn't surprise me." She linked an elbow with each young man, pulling them toward the door. "How else could you have received the best marks in class?"

Robert raised an eyebrow, unable to let the remark slide. "As I recall, your name was as often at the top of the class as mine."

"Yes." She waved her head airily. "But that made sense."

"I am insulted." Robert put on a look of mock offense. "You may receive my forgiveness by holding the door for my cousin and me."

Chris reached a hand toward the latch, and Robert slapped it away. His cousin pretended to reel back from the sheer force of the slap by flinging himself against the wall. "I wouldn't if I were you, Aurelia," Chris teased, getting into the spirit of the conversation. "With a friend like him, you might not come back in one piece." The words slipped like a shadow into Robert's mind.

Aurelia swung open the door. "I do this not for your forgiveness, but because I have no wish to argue until the festivities are over. Let's get on with it, shall we?"

"Hear, hear!" Chris chimed in.

Aurelia hoped Chris would manage to help her escape the palace grounds without turning it into a performance. As they approached the front gate, he took off his mask and slung out a hand in a casual greeting. "Hey, Filbert, seen any dangerous characters pass through here tonight?"

Filbert grinned, failing to ask the identity of the rooster's companions. "Not as terrifying as you." He reached out a hand as if to pluck a feather from Chris's plumed tail.

"Test not my fowl wrath!" Chris jerked away, pushing Aurelia and Robert before him and herding them to safety. Soon all three friends wound down the sloping road without an armed escort.

"Who was that at the gate?" Robert asked. "He looked quite familiar."

"Daria's brother," Aurelia explained. "You might not have known him very well. He joined our class after you left."

"But isn't he a couple years older than we are?" Robert asked.

"Three years," Chris said, "and even at that, he barely managed to complete his course work. He has a good aim with a rifle, and he's loyal. You couldn't get him to criticize His Majesty even in jest. But he's not the brightest fellow to ever stand a post."

Just the type of man my father promotes, Aurelia thought, *someone who does what he is told without asking questions.*

"It was fortunate for us, then, that he was at the gate," Robert said.

Chris clapped a hand to his chest in mock agony. "You question my skill, cousin. I could have talked us through that gate with the king himself standing guard. Filbert just allowed me to reserve my wit for more important challenges."

The three companions paused at the bottom of Palace Hill to take in the festive view. Dusk was creeping over the city,

and the excitement in the air grew with the approaching darkness. Painted lanterns hung from tree limbs in a shimmering
palette. Revelers swept along in costumes even more varied
than the lanterns. Judges in black robes brushed elbows with
thieves dangling fake jewels and pocket watches. From peddlers
to princes, banshees to bats, nightingales to nursery rhyme
characters, nothing within imagination's realm was off-limits.
The only common factor was that every face wore a mask:
masks of cloth, seeds, feathers, papier-mâché, and dozens of
other materials. Some scarcely surrounded the eyes. Others
completely covered faces.

Perhaps no one wanted to remain anonymous as much as
Aurelia. In disguise, she was simply another person enjoying
the magic of the evening. Men and women welcomed her as an
equal, slapping sugary drinks and alcoholic concoctions into her
hands. She drank the punch and passed Chris the alcohol.

The crowds thickened as they neared the corridor leading
to the city center. The wealthiest families owned the buildings
lining this road, and the most exquisite of these homes were
brightly lit. Scarves draped down from balconies, and wreathes
of flowers graced the necks of garden statues. Windows and
doors had been thrown open, causing the mingling of rich
smells and music: baked chocolate with violin chords, orange
peels with flute solos, maple syrup with string quartets—a waft-
ing swirl of enticement.

Aurelia, Chris, and Robert drifted from house to house, dancing at parties, tossing rings and darts in games of chance, and
sampling salty-sweet pretzels dipped in melted chocolate.

Eventually they joined in a group of singers following a small
band of walking musicians and tumbling performers. This
group wound its way around several city blocks, then formed a
large circle under the cherry blossoms by the great marble fountain. The singing grew louder as a crowd already at the fountain
joined in. The performers led everyone in five or six more songs
before guiding the entire group into a tavern.

As Aurelia and her friends waited for crowd members to
pass in front of them, a girl wearing a sleek black dress and the
fabric wings of a starling crashed into Chris. Her mask consisted
of little more than purple heart-shaped patches worn around
the eyes. Recognizing her at once as one of Melony's friends
from court, Aurelia hoped the recognition was not mutual.
Fortunately, the starling did not look in her direction. Giggling
up at Chris, the girl tapped him on the shoulder.

Chris encircled the starling's thin waist with his bare arm.
"How did you find me?" he asked.

Giggling again, the sound grating on Aurelia's nerves, the starling said, "I know you well enough not to fall for that disguise. I'm
afraid you were not raised to blend in." She slid her hand up to
caress Chris's face.

Oh, please. The falseness behind the starling's voice and
actions made Aurelia want to strike her with a talon or two.

Shooting Chris a knowing look, she tugged Robert away, calling over her shoulder, "Let's leave these two lovebirds alone."

Together, she and her remaining companion struggled through the cluttered streets. They wove around vendors' stalls for a while. But Aurelia had already drained the slim purse she had bothered to bring along, and Robert had no need for glass beads or decorative weavings. The tight crowd and combined smell of food and drink grew stifling.

They stopped to catch their breaths beside the large fountain depicting rearing horses. Robert knelt as if to help her mount one of the magnificent stone steeds. She took his hand and climbed up to walk along the fountain's circular rim.

"Away, away!" shouted a man wearing a dark mustache and holding a painter's palette. Aurelia realized she had interfered with his portrait of a pair of revelers posing beside the fountain. He waved a paintbrush in anger, splattering red drops all over the white costume fabric of his paying customers.

Apologizing and smothering her laughter, Aurelia steered Robert away from the crowds, back toward the river. "I've had enough." She sighed as they wound their way up along the bank beside a curtain of willow boughs.

Nodding his approval, Robert walked beside her without speaking. The celebration sounds dimmed, and the number of paper lanterns decreased until only a scattering lit their way. He moved out on a carved bridge and leaned over the edge. People who did that always made Aurelia nervous, but she forced herself to hold her tongue, having learned from experience that protest only encouraged them.

He pulled back slowly, continuing to gaze down at the dark water and the reflection of a single lantern's light. "This is what I missed the most," he said, startling her by breaking the companionable silence. "The river. I always felt so connected with it, connected with the world here on this bridge."

Hearing him voice her feelings made her uneasy. "But now you've seen the world," she said, unable to keep the envy out of her voice.

"Only another corner of it and the route on the way there." He turned around, resting his elbows on the railing and peering up at the patch of sky above his head. "I think the more you see, the more you realize you have yet to see."

"You sound like our old instructors." She wrinkled her nose. "The more you learn—"

"The more you realize how much you don't know," Robert finished for her. "Chris said you aren't taking classes anymore. I always assumed you'd attend university, or at least have the professors come to you."

She choked over her father's words as she voiced them. "Apparently I can better serve my kingdom if I commit my time in more useful ways." She knew the darkness could not hide the bitterness and disappointment in her voice. A variety of threats, bribes, and frequent reminders about her duty had conspired to keep her watching as other classmates went on to join the university ranks.

To Robert's credit, he attempted a switch to a less sensitive topic. "Who was the girl who approached Chris back there? You seemed in a hurry to avoid her."

"Hmm." This was no more an enjoyable subject but encouragingly less personal. "Tedasa. She is a friend of Melony's and one of the most eligible young ladies at court." Aurelia did not bother to keep the sarcasm out of her voice.

He laughed. "I've rather been enjoying the company of an eligible lady all evening."

"Ah, you are mistaken," Aurelia corrected him. "One thing I have not been all evening is a lady. That is why it has been enjoyable."

"Nonetheless." He refused to let the subject drop. "You did not seem inclined to spend any more time in our unexpected companion's presence than you had to."

Aurelia was uncomfortable sharing her honest opinion when she knew it might get back to Chris.

"She didn't go to school at the palace with us," Robert prompted.

"Her father is a foreign dignitary. He spends his time traveling. When her mother died last year, he rescued his society daughter from the wealthy boardinghouse where she was staying and brought her to court."

"You're still not telling me why you dislike her." Robert tapped the bridge railing with the flat of his hand.

Exasperated, Aurelia gave in. "She lives and breathes her father's money. If your cousin doesn't watch himself, he'll find she's built her nest right on top of his inheritance. She's not just another lady's maid he can dangle without consequences."

"Jealous?" There was an odd tone in Robert's voice.

"Hardly." Aurelia scolded him with her eyes. "I don't like people being used, especially those I care about."

Robert leaned back to peer up at the sky. "I wouldn't worry about Chris. I can't imagine him doing anything as respectable as courting a wealthy debutante."

"He didn't seem that worried about spreading his feathers for her tonight." The sarcasm was back in her voice. *An unattractive habit*, she thought. *I ought to correct it.*

Robert smiled. "Ah, but then you see, he didn't; a rooster did. You are not the only one capable of walking that hazy tightrope."

"If you stay on the tightrope long enough, sooner or later you are going to fall."

"Enough," he said. "When the conversation has dwindled to metaphors, it is time to find a new topic."

"You say that only because you were losing your argument."

"Who says that every point of a discussion has to be an argument?"

"No one." She grinned. "But with you it always is."

"Only when I'm talking to you."

He was telling the truth. Most of her memories of him involved verbal debate, whether during class discussions, in-depth study sessions, or casual conversations. She and Robert were too much alike: competitive, intrigued by new ideas, and determined not to give in when they felt they were right. What saved them from hating each other was that they could each be persuaded to change sides when confronted with a strong enough argument. Perhaps that was why they enjoyed debating so much. There was always a chance either might persuade the other to take up his or her case.

"Fine, then, let's talk about you," she suggested, both because she was curious about his new life and because she did not want the conversation to loop back to her. "What is life on the frontier like?"

He shrugged. "It's a lot of hard work, but I like it. Not the farm-ing that much. Father and I also train horses. The stubborn ones enjoy trying to land me on the ground, which is how I get the bruises I mentioned last night. Still, there's always a need on the frontier for a good mount."

She nodded to show she was listening and did not want to interrupt.

"The life suits my parents," he continued. "I think they are happier having their own place, something they've worked to build. It may not rival the palace for glory and comfort, but they have each other."

"And control over their own destiny." She could not keep the longing from her voice.

"Exactly," he said. "I think that's why they wanted to leave. They'll never come back. I'm not sure they could even be persuaded to visit."

That surprised her. "Not even to see family? You don't think your father will ever visit your uncle again?"

"I guess Father thinks Uncle Henry is just as capable of coming to see him, and I doubt it would ever occur to Uncle Henry to travel to the frontier."

Aurelia blushed. She supposed Robert was right. Travel without roads was too difficult, and the rugged land was too sparsely populated to ensure safety for a lost or weary traveler. No one she knew would consider the trip unless he or she had plans to live there. It had never occurred to her that people on the frontier might feel just as reluctant to make the same journey in reverse.

"But *you* came," she said.

"Yes." The clipped response indicated he was not going to elaborate.

"Do you think you'll want to stay there? On the frontier, I mean."

"I don't know. How do I know if it's where I really want to live when there are so many places I've never been?"

Envy congealed inside her. She could imagine it in her veins, an ugly green-and-purple acid squeezing her heart and lungs.

Don't, she thought, trying to push it away. *Don't think about things you can't have. It will just make you miserable.* "You'd like to travel, then?"

"If I can find a way to make a living at it for a while." He smiled wryly. "I'm not inclined to be a soldier, and I can't imagine I'd make much of a peddler seeing as I don't like asking for anyone's hard-earned coin."

They lapsed into silence, and Robert tilted his head back up at the cloudy sky. "That I don't miss," he said so softly she suspected the words were more for him than for her.

"What?"

He took a moment to answer. "The sky here is always overcast, like it can't let the sun out more than a day."

"It's past midnight." She looked at him, confused. "There'd be no sunlight anyway."

"True, but on the frontier there are enough stars to restring a broken soul." He dropped his gaze back to her. "It must sound silly to you, being used to this, but the clouds make me feel closed in now. I miss seeing the sky and the sense of space I have out there."

"I wish I could see it."

Her words seemed to startle him out of his reverie. "Why don't you go, then? It will all be under your leadership someday. Shouldn't you find out about it?"

"Yes, I should." The words came out choppy and harsh. Must he bring up all her failures in one night? "Life isn't always as you'd imagine it, Robert!" She brushed past him, making her way across the bridge.

He moved to follow, but she faced him, her flat palm ordering him to stop. Something must have convinced him to obey. He turned back to the bridge rail, staring out over the river's voiceless waters. She left him there and crossed the bridge into the night, allowing her anger and frustration to spill off into the darkness, where it could burn without scarring anyone else.

Robert remained by the railing less than a minute, giving Aurelia time to get off the bridge though not out of eyesight. Obviously more was wrong with her than she let on. He knew he was capable of setting off her temper, but he had been teasing her all night without gaining so much as a glimmer of genuine anger. This time he had not been teasing at all, just asking a simple question.

If he waited until she calmed down, she might tell him something; but the chance was gone for tonight, the comfortable conversation scattered like Carnival leftovers on the ground. Besides, did he really want to be Aurelia's confidant? The part of his life dealing with the problems of the aristocracy was past him. He did not need to involve himself in the princess's minor problems. His job was to deal with the major one.

The memory of the attempted poisoning from the night before flashed into his mind. He could not let her walk alone, no matter how angry she was with him. Pushing himself away from the bridge rail, he started after her as she fumed her way around a curve on the opposite edge of the road.

He had just crossed over to the same side when a screaming sound yanked his attention. Horses? Robert's head snapped up in astonishment, searching for the source. It was the same sound mustangs made on the frontier when there was a fierce storm coming. *What under the clouds…?*

At that moment the distraught horses came careening around the corner, six of them pulling a carriage. Light flared in multiple pairs of wide eyes. Broken stones ricocheted out from the squealing wheels, and a man perched motionless in the driver's seat. The carriage, the horses, and the man's clothes were all black, fading into the night's cloak. Robert took in the scene, reaching past his fear to record finer details even as his body broke into motion.

Aurelia had already turned and was running back toward him. What happened next was instinct. He grabbed her by the hand, hauling her off the road toward the cliff bank. Somewhere his mind registered that the horses were also departing the roadside, coming after them. In swift movements, he swung Aurelia over the bank, watched her secure a grip, and slid over the edge. Somehow his hands grasped hold of the rocky surface, keeping his body from crashing into the river below.

The lead horses reared overhead, screaming shrilly enough to shred veins. Hooves slammed down on the earth, sending a cascade of small stones over the two humans clinging to the cliff side. Robert closed his eyes and pressed his face close to the earth. Dirt burned in his lungs, but he held his position until the pelting ceased.

When he opened his eyes, the horses were gone. He turned immediately to the presence on his right. Aurelia's chest heaved beside his. Her breath came out in rasping gulps, and her fingers clung to the rocky bank just as fiercely as his own. She was still alive. But the fear pounding through his body was so over-powering, there was no room for a sense of relief.

Chapter Four
HORSEFLESH

ROBERT PACED ON THE PRACTICE-YARD SAND, HIS boots tracing and retracing their own prints. He frowned at the gray clouds blocking out most of the morning light, though at least here he had space to think. Visions of the carriage attack had pressed down on his mind ever since he had scrambled up the riverbank the night before at Aurelia's side.

A team of six horses. All black, but none the same. His father had taught him nothing was identical. A spy must look beyond the similarities. Details and differences, those were the clues to identification. No knife, no sword, no carriage was exactly like another.

Robert had noted the height, approximate weight, and style of the carriage. At the pace it had been traveling, it was plenty large enough to overrun another vehicle on the road. He might trace the carriage or the carriage maker, but Robert had seen no crest or distinguishing features. He hoped if he spotted the exact vehicle, he could identify it. Still, he doubted the carriage was the best place to focus his attention.

He should have far better luck tracing the horses. Six black. Robert had spent the past four years working with horses on the farm. He loved their personalities, had spent hours studying their traits and learning to appreciate each as an individual. When the carriage had come into view, Robert's attention had focused on the horses. Both members of the lead pair were big, one with a large scar below the knee, the other with a long neck and shaggy coat. He had only caught a glimpse of the back four, but it had been enough to recognize two mares in the rear and two stallions, smaller than the lead pair, in the center. The mare on the right side had a white streak in her mane.

Someone had worked hard to put that team together. The horses had run full speed toward Aurelia and Robert, not shying at the nearness of the cliff. No animal would voluntarily charge itself into harm's way, despite the guise of the driver losing control. Those horses had been following instructions, obedient to the point of self-endangerment. They were a frightfully well-trained team. Robert would find all the horses together. And if they were together, he was certain he could identify them.

He also thought he could recognize the stallion with the scar even without the company of the other horses. It had led the charge and seemed to aim deliberately for Robert and Aurelia. A shiver ran down Robert's body. He could not shake the chilling feeling the stallion had done this before, charging and trampling the life from its victim. He had known many horses during his life: friendly, gentle, shy, cocky, proud, and wild—but he had never before seen one that was cruel. That horse had been hunting him last night. He would recognize it if he saw it again.

And he knew a horse and a team like that would leave an impression on anyone experienced with horses.

Who here would be? Of course, there was the head groom, but asking a palace insider would be risky. Outside of Chris, Uncle Henry, and the king, no one in the palace knew Robert's real purpose there. One leading question in the wrong quarters and his secret would be splashed about with the washwater.

No, he could not ask Daria's father. Robert needed someone in the city, someone who had access to wealthy houses and wealthy horses. He could ask Chris, but Chris had never cared much for horses. And Robert doubted his cousin was yet awake after the late Carnival night.

"Her Royal Highness, Princess Aurelia, wishes to see you, sir." A feminine voice tore through his mental web.

Robert flinched, caught unaware by the presence of a young lady's maid standing not ten feet before him. Hazel eyes stared through him as if they could read his thoughts. "Is something wrong?" he asked, worried Aurelia had realized the carriage accident was no accident.

"The royal physician has restricted Her Highness to her rooms for the day, and she is in search of entertainment."

Robert raised his eyebrows. He certainly had no intention of spending the day in Aurelia's rooms. He needed to find those horses.

On the other hand, he had to admit he wanted to see her, to see for himself that she was still alive this morning, unchanged. She had been in a hurry last night to return to the palace, too much of a hurry to let him comfort her, but he suspected underneath her urgency had been fear. He nodded and reached for his frock coat. "I suppose I can see her for a few minutes."

"Follow me, sir." The girl led him through a carved doorway and along the lengthy, formal route to Aurelia's rooms. The trip took forever. Men and women passed, pausing to offer a greeting. Robert struggled to identify each person's rank, his eyes seeking out the emblems, ribbons, and clothing that would tell him the correct means of response. He scrambled to remember titles and forms of address, all the while afraid he might offend someone. No wonder Aurelia had preferred traveling in disguise the previous night.

And now Robert was left with the guilt of having assisted in the secret escapade. Nothing about the previous night's attack made sense. How had she been recognized? They had overrated the strength of her disguise by half.

He should have informed palace security.

He should have warned his uncle.

He should have—

The rap of the lady's maid's knuckles on Aurelia's private door restrained his self-inflicted flogging. He had passed through the princesses' joined parlor without even realizing it.

"My lady, I am returned with Robert Vantauge," the girl said.

"Come in!" Aurelia called, then watched as Robert entered the sitting room. *Come in and let slip everything your uncle told you.* Her various attempts to speak with her father about last night's accident had resulted in a dearth of answers, an excess of concern, and her following confinement in the name of good health. She was being kept out of the investigation for some reason, and Robert must know more than she did.

His blue eyes studied her with intensity. "Are you all right?" he asked.

She had the sudden sharp memory of his hands lifting her from the cliff and pulling her to him. An unnatural warmth rushed up to her cheekbones.

She tried to shake off the thought by pointing dramatically at the chair across the table from her seat. "Care to test me?" She lifted a card deck from the game table's patterned surface and shuffled.

He slid into the empty giltwood chair.

"Keep your wits about you, sir," she heard Minuet whisper. "I have heard Her Highness is not one to lose a card game on purpose."

"I'll keep that in mind," Robert replied.

Aurelia dealt the cards. Then, hoping he might let down his guard, she eased the conversation smoothly onto the topic of horses. A brief summary of Robert's recent equestrian experiences grew into a winding pathway of horse breeding, training techniques, and the relationship between horse and rider. By the time he admitted surprise at her expertise with regard to both horses and cards, she had trounced him in three straight hands of double hearts.

She used the compliment as a chance to launch her interrogation. "I thought I was familiar with the strongest teams in the city, but I didn't know the one we ran into last night. Tell me, Robert. What is being done about that carriage? Has the driver been identified?" She glanced up to gauge his reaction.

Robert fumbled, cringing as a jack of diamonds fell faceup on the table. "Why would anyone tell *me*?"

She gave him a penetrating look. "Because your uncle is the king's adviser, your father was a spy, and you were there last night. Don't tell me you haven't asked." She sloughed a high card. "What does Chris say?"

"I doubt Chris will say anything for several hours yet. He's still asleep."

The lie was so unexpected Aurelia had no idea how to react. True, she had feared Henry might tell his nephew not to discuss the accident with her until the investigation was complete, but why would Robert lie over something as trivial as Chris's whereabouts? It *was* a lie, though. She had already seen Chris that morning, laughing with Tedasa in the parlor.

"Asleep?" She gave Robert the chance to correct himself.

"As a drunken rooster."

"Don't play verbal games with me." She slapped another high card on the table. "That driver on the road last night came around the corner in a reckless manner. He or she should have reported the incident to the authorities."

Robert picked up the card with a painful slowness and began a new round. "I would have thought so myself, but nothing has been reported. Apparently the driver does not want to be identified."

Doubt spiked through her chest. If Robert had lied about Chris, he might be lying now. "Then we must see that the driver is found," she snapped. "He or she shouldn't be allowed to endanger other lives."

"I agree. However, I doubt the palace guards have enough time to investigate the disappearance of a reckless carriage driver. Perhaps I should ask in the city myself. I believe I could describe the horses well enough so someone who knows them might recognize them."

"I suppose that would be a decent start," she acknowledged grudgingly.

"You don't know who in the city might be a good horseman

or horsewoman to ask?" Robert probed. "Perhaps someone familiar with the upper classes as well as the horses that come in and out of the city gates?"

She floundered, not able to come up with an ulterior motive behind his offer. "There are several people," she finally said, then gave him the best suggestion she could, "but I'd start with Drew Fielding. Daria's father asks him for breeding advice, and I know Drew advises many upper-class families looking for strong teams. He runs the gamut on horseflesh. Spends plenty of time fleecing commoners at the city racecourse as well. And he'd probably like to talk to you anyway. He loves to hear about horse breeding in other regions of the kingdom."

The clock chimed eleven and Robert stood up. "Listen, if I'm going to go find this Fielding, I need to leave." He placed the winning card on the table. An ace of hearts.

She stared, stunned, unable to shake the feeling that he had won more than the game.

Twenty minutes later, a commoner rode out through the palace gates.

At least he was dressed as a commoner. Comfortable in his own worn shirt, trousers, and buckskin jacket, Robert guided his personal mount onto a dirt trail skirting the western half of Tyralt City. According to a talkative groom, the place to be was a local horse fair, and Robert assumed Drew Fielding would be there.

The fairgrounds were located in the northeast corner of town, not far from the main gate. Robert could have walked straight there as quickly as he could ride around the city circumference, but he preferred to avoid the heavy traffic of wagons and carriages cluttering the main road.

The famous Tyralian wall rose up on his left, its protective layers of stone reaching as high as the palace tower. The wall swept out from behind the palace, traced its way down the slope and around the front of the city, disappeared along the waters of the bay, and climbed back up the hill to complete the circle. Tyralian peasants had built the wall more than five hundred years before, and Robert pitied the invading armies that had broken themselves and their weapons upon the impenetrable stone.

His horse, Horizon, broke into a canter beside the wall's edge, and Robert allowed the three-year-old stallion to enjoy the run down the sparsely populated slope before pulling his mount to a safer brisk walk at the edge of the marketplace. The powerful bay slowed reluctantly, and Robert maintained a firm grip for the next hundred feet. Horizon was not opposed to depositing a rider on the ground when asked to do something unpleasant.

The marketplace eventually gave way to tenement buildings. Grim faces stared out from rickety staircases and stained windows. Robert guided Horizon closer to the Tyralian wall, hoping to avoid the downward path of refuse or emptied bedpans. Broken carts and wagon pieces littered the alleyways, and dirt smeared everything, even the wet laundry connecting each row of buildings with the next.

"Excuse me, mister, do you have a coin to spare?" A ragged boy stretched out a hand toward Horizon. The stallion backed away, and Robert leaned forward to press a few coins into the grimy palm.

A sudden flood of skinny bodies with outstretched hands scrambled out from behind corners and doors. Children surrounded him, pressing close, with no regard for their own safety in the face of the stallion's sharp hooves. Robert struggled to calm his horse as high voices raised in begging pleas.

"A copper! A copper!"

"For my family, mister."

"For my hungry baby sister."

"Please, mister."

"Please, please!"

He emptied his pocket and shouted a warning to the children before urging Horizon forward. Robert felt thankful when the inns and taverns near the main gate replaced the tenements. He had seen poverty before. No one on the frontier had much in the way of material goods, but here the poverty felt raw, the lives of the poor standing out in stark contrast to those of the nearby aristocracy.

Horizon whistled with excitement as he passed the city stables and approached the horse fair. A roped-off boundary came into view, and Robert dismounted, shortening the reins.

He had no intention of providing a horse thief with the lift of a lifetime.

Robert descended into the fair's shifting sea of shoving elbows and stomping boots. Cajoling voices of horse traders glided under the demanding questions of potential buyers. Prices swung like dying pendulums, the distance between both ends narrowing toward the center. Unbridled children, grown feral with their parents' neglect, pounded after one another, ducking dangerously under horses and humans alike, then popping up just long enough to spot their fellow predators and prey. Draped over everything hung the humid smell of hay, manure, and horseflesh.

Robert strained to identify a horse worth the attention of a genuine horseman. Filtering through dozens of pack and cart horses, he focused on a full team tied to a single hitching post. Here, at least, was a place to start.

Passing an elderly man swamped with questions from interested customers, Robert approached a skinny girl standing in the background. The girl's dress was smeared with dirt and her shoes were covered in manure; but her head was up, and her eyes were watchful. She had spotted his approach before he opened his mouth, and she eyed him as if she thought he might be planning to pilfer her charges. "Excuse me, miss," he inquired. "Could you tell me where I might find a man named Drew Fielding?"

"Drew?" She arched an eyebrow. "Well, we haven't seen much

of him this mornin', but he shouldn't be difficult to find. He doesn't blend into the crowd, does he?" Her eyes danced.

"He doesn't?" The comment aroused Robert's curiosity. "I'm afraid I don't know him. In what way does he stand out?"

The girl grinned cheekily. "Well, if you haven't met him, it wouldn't do much good to explain. I would head over toward the plum tent in the center of the field." She motioned toward a bright purple tent about a hundred feet behind her. "He's wearin' a black hat today with a red feather in it. That ought to be enough information for you to find him."

With thanks for her help and a renewed sense of curiosity, Robert plunged back into the crowd. He emerged close enough to the purple tent to see a lopsided group gathered around a table in the violet shade. On one side of the table, six or seven people collected coins and jotted down information from the swarm on the other side. *A gambling center,* Robert decided.

The sight of a vocal crowd member ripped all other thoughts from his mind. The man's head towered eight to ten inches above the throng, and on it rested a roguish black hat graced with an ostentatious red feather. This, then, must be Drew Fielding.

Robert had to laugh when he thought of the girl's taunting comment about this man not blending in. He certainly did not.

In fact, Drew resembled nothing so much as Robert's childhood impression of a gentleman pirate. His skin was charcoal black and gleamed against a silk shirt, tight vest, and tawny trousers. With the exception of a pair of grass-stained boots, the entire outfit shone spotless despite the chaotic surroundings. Tied securely back, the man's dark hair hung below his shoulders, and a single ruby earring sparkled from his left ear.

Robert found himself conceding yet another round to Aurelia. She might have mentioned that the man stood out from the general populace like a bird of paradise in a daisy patch.

Suddenly the flamboyant horseman appeared at Robert's side or, rather, appeared directly in front of Horizon. The man's eyes assessed the stallion, gliding over the black mane, drifting along the sleek red neck, halting on the powerful chest and shoulder muscles, sliding down the smooth forearms and over the black lower legs.

"I say, lad, fresh off the frontier, eh?" Fielding said.

Robert chafed at the moniker, but adopted a slight frontier drawl and replied, "Fresh enough." The horseman could not be fifteen years his elder.

"Interesting mount you have here. Thinking of trading him for something better for the city?"

Don't you wish. "Matter of fact, I've seen an interesting stallion. Thought maybe someone here could direct me to the owner."

Fielding's head snapped back. "Someone direct you to me, did they? And here I thought I was the one who started this conversation."

"Hmm," Robert replied, "I thought a fine horse was the only

thing could start a conversation with a fine horseman."

The wary look disappeared from the other man's eyes and a loud laugh whooshed out of his lungs. At Robert's shoulder, Horizon snorted in response and took a step back. Fielding moved a step forward, keeping his short distance from the stallion. "Now, that's a truth I can't deny." He met the horse's stare. "You are the one who started this conversation."

Without breaking his gaze with Horizon, Drew spoke again to Robert. "All right, lad, I'll direct you to this stallion that's caught your interest, in exchange for a little information about your mount here. What do you say?"

"Fair enough."

"Not here, though." Drew gestured to the left. "I've had enough time in these crowded surroundings. Let's have a drink in my tent and share our information in a more comfortable location."

Robert looked up hesitantly at Horizon. "I'm not leaving him alone, nor in anyone else's charge."

Drew slapped Robert on the back. "Can't say I blame you, lad. Got to admit I'd be tempted to make off with him myself. If you can control him, bring him right into the tent with you. It's big enough, and we can't be excluding him from the conversation anyway, now, can we?"

The noisy crowd parted magically as Fielding led the way toward a white canvas tent propped on ten-foot poles. The heavy canvas draped to the ground on three and a half sides, with one corner flung up to provide a doorway.

Horizon balked at the tent flap. Powerful chest muscles rose above Robert's head as the stallion reared, threatening the entire structure. Drew moved to help, but Robert stopped him. "Hold back. He's not reliable with strangers." As the stallion dropped down, Robert grabbed the side of the bridle and glared at his mount. Cocky horse came all the way through the crowd but chose this moment to attract attention.

Confident that Horizon was finished with his minor revolt, Robert guided him into an almost barren retreat. Several folded wooden chairs rested against the pole by the opening, and a painted white box stood two feet high in the center of the tent like an ivory monument.

Fielding set up his own chair beside the box and motioned for Robert to do the same. *Not too much of a gentleman to do his own work and not enough of a gentleman to do the work of others.*

While Robert struggled to find a smooth surface for his own chair, his host slipped a hand into the box and produced a bottle of cheap white wine.

Robert shook his head.

The man reached back in and took out a bottle of Favinoit. Robert struggled not to grin. Drew placed a glass in front of his guest.

"No, thank you." Robert said, fully aware he was rejecting the best wine in the kingdom. "Too early in the day for me." He never drank alcohol but found this response gained fewer comments.

Fielding arched an eyebrow but put the extra glass away and motioned toward Horizon. "Well then, *lad*, to our discussion. Where'd you find this temperamental masterpiece?"

"Raised him myself, on the frontier."

Robert launched into his own question without pause. "I'm looking for a big black stallion, saw him leading a team of six." Leaving out all the circumstances of his observation, he went on to describe the stallion with the scar, the other team members, and the carriage. "Seemed like that stallion would do anything for his driver," Robert ended. "Put his life in danger charging right up to the edge of a cliff, just shifting direction at the last moment."

Throughout the explanation, Drew remained silent, seating himself in his chair. He now pushed the chair back, away from Robert. "Noticed that, did you?" Drew said. "And that devotion to the driver attracted you to that horse?" He took a deep breath. "Well, lad, I can tell you here and now you aren't going to talk the owner out of that stallion. Might sound hard, but there's more to a good horse than obedience. If you think obedience without common sense makes a fine mount, you'll never be much of a horseman."

Ignoring the slight, Robert goaded, "How can you be sure I can't get the horse if you don't know who the owner is?"

"Here now." The older man leaned back, propping his boots up on the white box. "I didn't say I don't know the owner. It's because I *do* know the owner, and the horse as well, that I told you what I just did. That team belongs to the queen's own stables. Not at the palace, but her personal stables back in Midbury. Nobody but the queen herself selects those horses."

Crash!

Noise clattered through the tent. Drew and Robert sprang to their feet, whirling to face the entryway. Scattered at the foot of the tent pole lay the remaining foldable chairs, toppled from their perch. Standing above them in the open doorway was Aurelia Lauzon, princess of Tyralt, her face drained of color except for the streak of a bulging red vein running from jaw to collarbone.

Chapter Five

HONESTY

THAT TEAM BELONGS TO THE QUEEN'S OWN STABLES. Drew's words repeated in Aurelia's mind, penetrating her thoughts, her conscience, her self-control. There was something ominous about that team. She could not shake the image of those broad black chests and pounding hooves. *Nobody but the queen herself selects those horses.*

"Aurelia?" Robert said.

"Well, if it isn't Her Majesty in the flesh, or rather in disguise," Drew boomed, referring to the white cap, baggy shirt, and worn trousers adorning her body.

Robert stared at her as if in shock. No doubt he was. But his shock paled in comparison to hers. She had tried to convince herself that his lie about Chris was not important; but now she saw it for what it really was, a small slip in an attempt to hide a larger truth that the accident had been no accident. Her instincts were correct. The horses had charged. And those horses belonged to the queen. Aurelia could not deal with the implications, not while Robert was staring at her. She whirled and fled.

"Aurelia, wait!" She could hear Robert coming after her. "Wait!"

Her lithe body slipped into the crowd, and she took advantage of the chaos filling the path. Dodging water troughs, bales of fresh hay, and picnic supplies, she zigzagged through the fairgrounds. Twice she thought she had lost him only to have his dark head flash into view.

Perhaps he would give up in the tangle of side streets. She burst from the crowd, ducked under the rope barrier, and darted into an alley, where her strategy unraveled. Once he was free of the throng, Robert's speed and stamina became a factor. The thudding of his footsteps sped up and, less than five buildings down, a strong hand closed around her upper left arm and swung her to a halt. She fought for a second, gave up, and rested her hands on her hips.

For minutes they just breathed, measuring each other with their eyes. She struggled to gain a grasp on her senses. "All right, you stopped me. Now talk." He was the one who should have something to say. Not only had he lied to her, but judging from what she had overheard, he had lied to Drew as well.

Robert glanced down the empty street as if searching for an answer, then stated the obvious in a controlled voice. "I want to know why you ran away just now." Still avoiding the truth. Well, he should not have bothered to come after her, then.

"And you thought chasing me down and restraining me would explain that for you?" she snarled.

Kicking a piece of broken glass, he met her gaze. "I am more patient than you, Aurelia. I can wait here all day."

The comment needled her. He *would* wait there, pretending to be the one who did not know what was going on. She paced back and forth on the cobblestones, emotions warring in her chest. Fine, then. If he insisted on stating the obvious, she could as well. "I ran because I was angry."

He waited.

She took a rattling breath. "With you."

"Only with me?"

Another breath. The coolness of his question was maddening. "I don't know. Maybe someday you'll decide to tell me." The accusation sliced into the tight air.

For a moment his face flickered as if he was losing his sense of control, but the words coming from his mouth remained infuriatingly calm. "Let's retrace our day. I saw you this morning. We talked. You told me to ask Drew Fielding about horses. I looked up Mr. Fielding. You arrived, heard a few comments, and hurtled your way off the fairgrounds into an alley." He waited again.

How dare he patronize her? "Why don't you try that again? Maybe you'll achieve your goal of making me sound like the problem." Still he said nothing. She turned and began walking away. "Let me know when you feel like telling the truth. Otherwise enjoy your stay in the capital."

She walked slowly at first, trying her best to maintain an aura of calm, hoping deep down that he would stop her and admit he had lied. That he would apologize and tell her what he really knew about last night.

But he did not. And the disappointment and her anger at herself for feeling that disappointment were too much. She lurched into motion, pounding around dim corners and down musty streets. Taverns and boardinghouses ranged beside her, the sharp smell of alcohol emanating from their connected facades. The uneven surface of the streets challenged the strength of her ankles, and rough edges of broken cobblestones dug into her leather shoe bottoms.

A jagged pain in her side slowed her to a walk. Her earlier flight had cost her. She should not be running. For that matter, she should not be hiding and skulking in disguise. She was the future ruler of this city. She should be free to stroll its streets whenever she wanted. Aurelia kicked a broken stone into the gutter and watched it skid over the holes of a grate before plummeting into the sewer below.

Where to now? Not the palace. Not that gilt prison of her stepmother's with its tapestry barriers and filigree locks. The wharf seemed the ideal refuge, its port filled with ships headed for exotic lands such as the Outer Realms. To think, if she stowed away in one of those creaking hulls, she could set foot in a foreign country. The lure of the water pulled like a hook lodged in the tissue of her chest. Her steps quickened, and she lifted her head.

Away. She must get away from the suffocation of her life, the pressure to marry, and the people she could not rely upon. Every time she thought she could trust someone—

Aurelia brushed back the thought and the hurt that came with it. She must escape.

Robert wanted to leap after her, tell her she was not going to win by leaving. But the truth bound him in the alley. Clearly, she knew he had been keeping information from her, and whatever she knew was a long way from the whole truth. *If I stop her, what can I tell her?* He had been ordered not to inform her of the assassination plot. Ordered by the king. The king!

Her anger didn't bother him, but the hurt he had seen in her face did. That same look had gripped him in the tent earlier. He was unsure whether he could ... whether he should ... curse it! Suddenly he did not know anything.

Then a chill crackled through his body. While he had been standing still, thinking about his reaction to the argument, she had slipped off among the city streets alone—alone in a city she had nearly been killed in the night before.

He rushed to the end of the alley. Vacant walls and shuffling strangers met his gaze. Searching at random would be foolish. He had no idea where to look, and she did not want to be found, at least not by him. Hoping she was disguised as well as she believed, he plunged back into the fairgrounds, aiming for Fielding's tent.

The horseman was waiting for him, or rather he was still in his tent, talking with a restless bay stallion. Horizon snorted as Robert's head slipped under the heavy canvas flap. Drew straightened to his full height. "When I invited you in here, lad, I did not know I was signing up to watch over a horse."

Robert shrugged. "My apologies." He knew his hopes of being overlooked by this man were shredded. Aurelia trusted Drew. That much was clear; and based on the information the horseman had shared about the stallion, there was little chance Drew could be involved in the assassination plot. Robert resolved to open up as much as necessary if it would help him find the princess.

Keeping a hand wrapped around Horizon's reins, Fielding sat down, kicked his feet up on the white box, and gestured for Robert to take the other chair. "We have a discussion to resume. Thus far I've been doing all the talking, a point I failed to notice until you took off."

Determined not to waste time, Robert said, "I need to know where Aurelia might go in the city. She may be in danger."

"That girl?" Fielding scoffed. "If she ever was in danger, all she'd have to do would be to announce her real identity. Folks in the city would rather see her on the throne than her father. Without her as his heir, the king would have lost his hold on their loyalty years ago. She stole the people's hearts at the age of three when she threw herself on her brother's coffin at the state funeral. Besides, she can blend in with anyone."

Robert filed away Drew's comments, wondering how many enemies Aurelia had made in her unintended quest for popularity. "You're saying she does this often, coming into the city in disguise?"

Drew laughed. "She knows the veins of this city better than a street urchin."

"But how does she get out of the palace?"

"Lad, I can't tell you that. I can tell you the lass was raised by the palace staff. His Majesty never had time for her. For every guard keeping her in, there are three stable hands or kitchen maids or outside gardeners willing to smuggle her out."

"Can you tell me where she might go?" Robert pleaded.

Drew fiddled with Horizon's reins. "Maybe, if I start getting some answers."

"Ask your questions."

"All right, you show up here dressed like a commoner, but your mount there is worth a small fortune. Judging by your reaction earlier, you know the difference between Favinoit and your regular white wine. And you know Her Royal Highness well enough to call her by her first name. Who in the king's name are you?"

Robert told him.

"Vantauge?" The man drew out the surname. "You're related to the king's adviser?"

"He is my uncle. I came back to see him."

"And others, I presume." Drew's eyes sparkled. "I haven't seen a lad chase after a girl with such gusto in a long time."

Robert waited for the next question.

"And why should I tell you where the lass may be when she doesn't want to be near you? She deserves her moments of freedom. They're rare enough these days."

"I won't expose her. I just wish she'd asked me to come with her."

"Of course you do, lad." The teasing tone weighed heavy in Drew's voice. "Perhaps she didn't ask you because she doesn't trust you. She's had a rough time of it these last few years. Everyone views her through a spyglass, seeing how she can help them and losing perspective on the person."

"Everyone except you, you mean." Robert was less than tactful. The word *trust* had hit hard.

"Oh, I like the lass well enough, but I'm in her debt. I count on her support among the upper crust. There are those, even in the royal family, who find me"—he winked—"less than admirable."

Robert reworded his earlier question. "Where might she have gone?"

Drew wrapped the reins around his hand and released them, handing them to Robert. "I'm still waiting to hear about this beauty." The horseman rubbed Horizon's cheekbone. "But I can see it'll have to wait till later. The lass wanted to be shut of you, my boy. I shouldn't send you after her. On the other hand, I've chased my share of girls, and I reckon Miss Aurelia could do with a little chasing before she has to settle down for the good of the kingdom. She might have gone down to the docks. Has a dreamy fascination with far-off places."

Robert led the stallion out of the tent, and the horseman followed.

"I'll be checking in to hear about this horse," Drew said as Robert climbed on to the scuffed saddle. "He has a spirit I like. Not at all the type to obey just because his master says so."

Horizon broke into motion and headed through the thinning crowd, along the Tyralian wall, past inns and taverns, and out onto the wide crescent of the wharf. Gray-green water curved into the city port, its depth renowned along the southern coast as one of only two harbors navigable by large sailing ships. A bustling group of tan men dressed in duck cloth loaded goods on and off a brigantine vessel, but no white cap lingered nearby.

Dismounting, Robert walked along the edge of the bay toward a quieter section of the dock. Cool salt air filtered through tall masts and furled sails. The penetrating odor of raw fish drowned his nostrils. Water slapped a legato rhythm against the side of the dock, and shifting boards creaked accompaniment.

The sight of Aurelia perched on a barrel, one knee slung

over the other, eased his mind. She was safe for the moment. An old man with bushy eyebrows and a navy knit cap held the princess's attention. His ruddy fingers composed a fishing net, and his voice wrapped a hypnotizing rhythm around the lone listener.

Robert slid onto an empty barrel at Aurelia's side. She glanced at him, then turned her eyes out toward the bay. He struggled to reconcile her father's orders with his own emotions, but the sound of the seaman's voice soon overtook Robert's thoughts.

The man's story uncoiled, one thick, entrancing loop at a time. Despite having missed the beginning, Robert quickly captured the tale's essence because it matched historical fact. Two decades earlier, a ship carrying people from the Outer Realms had landed in port. The people, who spoke no Tyralian, had struggled to explain their need for help. Then the captain brought forward the body of a dead man bearing the pockmarks of disease. Fearing an epidemic, the king had denied the refugees assistance, ordering them to leave Tyralian waters.

In the seaman's story, however, a young boy from the Outer Realms named Andrew escaped the rigid guards and convinced the captain of another ship to help. After the forced departure of the refugees, this captain's ship followed, smuggling all the passengers safely onto Tyralian soil.

"And when you see a man or a woman of special height, there's a good chance he or she is from that same refugee ship."

The seaman tied a knot. "All thanks to a lad with the courage of a gull in a storm."

"Does that include you?" Aurelia asked, looking up into the man's wrinkled face.

The seaman uncurled himself from his seat and stood up. To Robert's astonishment, the man's head stretched above him almost as high as Drew's had earlier that afternoon. "Nay, lass." The man winked. "But I know the story to be true."

Aurelia laughed. "You know all stories to be true, even the one about the sea monster that swallowed the mermaid."

The man laughed, then stretched out a reddened palm toward Robert. "And who is this?"

"A friend," she mumbled.

"I enjoyed the story, sir, what I heard of it." Robert took the seaman's weathered hand, surprised at its strong grip.

"Aye, suppose you'll both be getting off before the sun goes down." The man tilted his head toward a sinking glow in the sky. A thin veil of clouds obscured the light's slow descent toward the western rim of the city wall.

"Yes, we should," Aurelia agreed. "Thank you again." As she hugged the wobbly seaman, Robert thought about the story. Law prevented any man, woman, or child of the Outer Realms from entering Tyralt. He wondered if the young boy named Andrew could be real, if a child truly had defied the king.

Then again, the young woman on his right was defying

that same king at this very moment. Robert doubted whether anyone had defied King Lauzon as often as she had. For all His Majesty's attempts to protect his daughter, here she was, standing on the wharf in boy's clothing, completely removed from her father's supervision. Robert was never going to be able to protect her if he followed the king's orders.

"Horizon can carry us both if you don't mind a few antics." Robert offered Aurelia his hand.

She gave him a critical look. "I'd rather walk."

"Then I'll walk with you. I need to tell you the truth."

She raised her eyes, seemed to accept the statement as a promise, and didn't argue as he fell into step beside her. The smell of fish faded as they moved up a quiet side street. Horizon's hooves clicked along the narrow stone surface and an uneasy silence descended. Robert struggled with how to begin.

"You were correct earlier about me not being entirely honest," he said.

She snorted, picked up her pace, and pulled away, a move he had seen from her once too often.

"Would you stop running?" Frustration cut through his voice. "You don't want to reach the palace too soon. I have a lot to say."

"Get on with it, then." She spun, scorn twisting her features as he stepped close. Dark eyes looked up, their depths filled with mixed emotions—anger and hurt, and deep down a layer of fear.

Holding her gaze, he grasped for words. "Over a month ago, Uncle Henry sent a letter, begging my father to return to the palace. In it he claimed the life of the heir to the throne was in danger."

She froze. "My life?" The emotions on her face clamped down.

"Yes." He watched her step away from him one careful stride, then turn to proceed slowly up the gentle curve of the street. She was no longer running.

As they walked side by side, he retraced the events of the last several weeks, telling her what he knew about all four assassination attempts. She listened without comment, guiding him from one street to the next, leaving behind the inns and taverns skirting the wharf and moving on to narrow alleys lining the backs of stores and merchants' shops. Supply barrels and wooden crates cluttered the path, and the smell of fired clay mingled with freshly baked bread.

Carriages did not come along these backstreets, but the citizens of Tyralt did. A trio of shoeshine boys drifted past, nibbling on rye bread. A middle-aged man carted a heavy load of dusty coal, and a group of gossiping women rushed forward, toting packages wrapped in brown paper. None of the passersby interrupted Robert's explanation. They each went about their business, paying no attention to the boy in the white cap and the commoner in frontier garb.

The muscles in Aurelia's face remained still. If anything,

her emotions became harder to read until Robert related his conversation with Drew. Then she shuddered. "I was afraid when I heard that," she said, "about the horse being from Elise's stables."

"Is that why you ran?" Robert asked.

"Yes, and because I was angry with you for lying."

"But you suggested I talk to Drew. How did you know I wasn't being honest with you?"

She let out a slow breath. "This morning when we were playing cards, you told me you couldn't ask Chris about the accident because he was sleeping. That's when I knew you were lying. I saw Chris this morning. He was in my parlor half an hour before I sent for you."

Of all the stupid ways to get caught in this deception. "What could possibly have motivated Chris to get up so early?"

"A starling with an excruciating voice. She was visiting Melony."

Robert groaned, then he refocused his thoughts on the scarred stallion's owner. Now that Aurelia knew the truth, he could ask her questions. "Do you believe there could be a connection between the queen and the assassination attempts?"

She eyed him, the screen over her emotions faltering. "I thought you were going to be honest with me. What *else* could it mean?"

"A number of things," he replied, "but that's not what I meant.

What is your first reaction? Does it seem plausible to you that the queen might be involved? Can you trust her?"

Aurelia trailed her fingers against a sandstone wall. "I don't know how anyone's attempts to murder me could be plausible. Elise and I have never been close. She made my father happy after my brother's death. Beyond that… she has always been Melony's mother, not mine." Her voice rose in anger. "But I hardly think that is a motive for murder. What reason could she have for wanting me killed?"

"If her daughter was in line for the throne, that might—"

"But the law forbids Melony from becoming queen."

"I know," he said. "And you've never felt threatened by your stepmother?"

Indecision flashed across her face, but she replied, "If I had ever felt I was in danger in the palace, I would not have kept quiet about the fact."

"I need you to stay quiet now, though." Intensity filled his voice. "To catch the person behind this, I need whoever it is to come into the open. The culprit must believe he or she is working in secret." Aurelia gave him an incredulous look. "Please," he begged. "Let me do my job. Don't say anything to the king yet. He did not want me to tell you about the danger. He didn't want you worried. I decided to tell you because I want you to be safe. I know you value your freedom, but I am asking you not to go out alone. If you must go, at least ask Chris or me to come with you."

"Chris?" She gave a half smile. "He has better things to do, like flirting with Melony's friends and lady's maids."

"Then ask me," Robert said. "I didn't come all this way to have you disappear on a city street somewhere."

Aurelia looked at him, an odd expression crossing her face. "Why did you come ... all this way?"

He stared at her, unsure what she was asking.

"Why are you here instead of your father?"

Robert felt his chest tighten. He thought about the day Uncle Henry's letter had arrived and the resulting conversation. The memory of that talk with his father still haunted him. Some truths Robert was not prepared to share.

Chapter Six
THE LETTER

THE SKY WAS BLUE THAT DAY, THE DAY UNCLE HENRY'S letter arrived. Blue and arching over the curved hilltops and rugged canyons of the frontier. The sun's rays had not yet chased away the chill of the morning air as Robert finished his chores and joined his father beside the corral to watch the approaching rider. A sturdy brown mustang followed the wagon tracks etched in the early spring grasses, and Robert recognized the mount of his closest neighbor to the east.

"Letter fer you, Brian," the neighbor said when he pulled up into the open space between the corrals and cabin. He rummaged in his bulky saddlebags and withdrew a thin brown envelope that he handed to Robert's father.

Mr. Vantauge ran his eyes over the writing on the sealed

parchment. He looked like an older version of his son, except for those eyes, which were brown and wary. "My thanks," he said. "Who can tell when I would have found the time for a trip to town?"

"Ya'll do the same fer me when ya do." The man closed the hide flap on his saddlebag. "Point of fact, I didn't pick it up in town. Ran into a lost-lookin' courier about five miles out. Asked me fer directions to the Vantauge homestead. He wasn't none too anxious to put that envelope into my care, but he finally handed it over after I explained he had another two days' travel with nary a man-made landmark for a stretch of ten miles." The neighbor coaxed his horse around in a circle. "Can't stay; seedin' still to do."

Robert's father nodded, his eyes once again drifting down to the letter. "Understood."

The neighbor touched his hat brim in a salute and retreated along the wagon tracks. A gust of wind blew over the plowed fields, sending a cloud of dust over the departing horse and rider, and the smell of fresh earth swept up to the corral where Robert stood peering over his father's shoulder.

VANTAUGE HOMESTEAD was printed across the paper in familiar handwriting.

Mr. Vantauge pulled away, walking toward the cabin. A twelve-foot wall of hewn logs formed the length of the building, and a sweet, vaguely off-key hum drifted out the lone window.

Robert slipped ahead, ducking under the low door frame. "There's a letter from Uncle Henry," he told his mother.

She set a soapy dish on the plain wood table and dried her hands on a cloth. Her blue eyes sparkled, and she pushed a loose strand of blond hair back under her scarf. "Really, Brian?" she said to her husband. "We had word from Henry only last month. He must miss you."

"More likely he is writing to ask why I haven't given up this 'foolhardy adventure' of mine yet." Robert's father winked as he slid onto a bench and cracked open the letter's wax seal. Gently he unfolded the wrinkled parchment.

Robert and his mother watched, eager to hear the news. Letters did not arrive often on the frontier, and letters from family were especially treasured. Mrs. Vantauge allowed the pewter mugs and wooden dishes to sit idle on the sideboard. Neither she nor her son made a sound.

Her husband's face darkened as he read. Instead of sharing the details or passing the precious paper to his wife, he folded the parchment and slipped it through the slit in his trousers into his pocket. Then, without looking up, he walked outside, leaving his audience in unfulfilled suspense.

Nothing more was said about the letter until dinner that night. Robert knew enough to let his mother handle the issue. She was the one with the gift for setting people at ease.

Mr. Vantauge sat down in his chair to a plate piled high with thick slices of roasted pheasant and homemade bread. Steam rose off the food, and the spicy scent of gravy filled the small room. "I could smell supper clear out in the barn," he said. "I haven't forgotten a special occasion, have I, Mary?"

Robert's mother set the flower-sprigged pitcher of milk on the table and smiled. "You have your son to thank for the fresh meat. He found the pheasant in one of your snares this morning." She lit a candle. "We thought you deserved a treat now you've finished the plowing."

"Still the seeding left." Mr. Vantauge plunged a fork into the white meat and began sawing away at it with his knife. "Cannot afford to wait for the weeds to begin to grow."

Mrs. Vantauge sat down, lifted her own fork, and asked gently, "Did Henry have anything of interest to discuss in his letter?"

The sawing knife froze. "He wants me to return to the palace for a while, but I have no intention of going."

"Why does he wish you to come?"

The muscles around Mr. Vantauge's mouth tightened. "We'll discuss it after dinner. I've had a long day and would prefer to eat in peace."

The cheery tone in the room disintegrated under his sullen stare. Robert and his mother exchanged brief looks. Tension clung to the dinner table, the participants holding themselves erect, each head, each shoulder, each arm suspended in the thick air. Utensils moved in slow motion lest they bang against a plate.

The slightest noise might tear a hole in the tablecloth of silence.

As the last bite disappeared from his father's dish, Robert slowly began to clear the table. He had no intention of leaving the cabin before the upcoming discussion.

Mr. Vantauge passed an empty mug to his son and pushed his chair back, but he did not get up. "Henry wants me to return to run an investigation. They've had four years to engage a new spy. I'm not responsible for their failure to do so. He's just going to have to do what he should have done before and hire someone to my old post."

Mrs. Vantauge nodded. "Yes, you're right." Her voice softened. "It must be important, though, if Henry asked you to come."

"He still thinks this venture is a phase I'm going through."

She nodded in sympathy, then prompted, "Did he explain the problem?" *Of course he did.* Robert watched his father. Uncle Henry could not ask his brother to travel halfway across the kingdom without stating the purpose, but Mr. Vantauge had never discussed a current investigation.

This night was different, though. Perhaps Robert's father felt he could talk about the case because he was not taking it. Perhaps he felt it was safe to share the details this far away from court, or perhaps he felt his son was now old enough to keep a secret. For whatever reason, the former spy relented. "My brother believes the life of the crown princess is in danger."

Blackness engulfed Robert's mind. Shock blocked out

everything except the crackle of parchment and Mr. Vantauge's voice reading the letter aloud.

The Palace, Tyralt City

XXV year of King Viry Lauzon

To Brian Vantauge,

I am writing you tonight not as your brother, but as the king's adviser. A week ago, a lady's maid found a silver goblet on the bedroom table of the crown princess. Not recognizing the snake mold entwined around the handle, the lady's maid informed me of the object. Its polish was laced with a deadly poison.

I began an investigation without success. The goblet has no signature and cannot be traced to any silversmith in Tyralt City. The placement of the poison suggests a hired assassin; however, this broadens the search for the actual instigator. Whoever the culprit, he or she has the money and power to hire someone inside the palace. This aspect of the plot concerns me the most and is the reason I have taken the desperate step of contacting you. The person who set the goblet on the table had access to the princess's bedchamber and has not been caught.

Please, Brian, as the king's royal spy of fifteen years, your knowledge and skill are unmatched by anyone on today's royal staff. I know you had your reasons for leaving, but I am asking you to return to the palace to help save the life of the princess. There is no reason to believe this assassination attempt will be the last.

With respect and love,

Henry Vantauge
King's Adviser

The words rebounded inside Robert's skull, faster and faster, slamming into all other considerations, grinding them to powder. "You could go," Robert said as his father refolded the paper. "I can complete the seeding myself."

"No!" Both his parents responded at once. Mr. Vantauge's chin jutted forward and Mrs. Vantauge gripped her husband's hand as if she could hold him there through sheer physical force.

"There is no telling how long the investigation might take or whether the effort would be successful," Robert's father argued. "I have given enough of my life to protect the royal family."

"Yes." Mrs. Vantauge turned over her husband's hand and slipped her own into the open palm. "And I've spent enough of my life waiting to see if my husband would survive his current investigation."

"I left for a reason." Robert's father ran a thumb along the back of his wife's hand. "And I'm not going back."

Robert swung his gaze between his parents. The strength of a promise made and a promise kept shone in both faces, impenetrable. "Then I will," he said, surprising himself with the statement.

"What?" Mr. Vantauge stood up. "You will *not*."

"Why not?" Robert replied, asking himself as much as his father. "I'm old enough to travel, and you don't really need me here."

"There's more than enough work on this place for both of us."

Robert felt his hands clench. He liked the homestead. He did. But he could not help feeling that it was his father's dream, not his. His voice rose. "You can't expect me to stay here forever."

"Robert." His mother's calm tone intercepted his anger. She knew how he felt, though he had not yet managed to broach the subject with his father. "Leaving the homestead is one thing. Returning to the palace as a spy is something else."

"It's my decision to make."

"Absolutely not," his father responded. "You have no experience running an investigation. You will get yourself killed."

Robert argued back "I'm not as well equipped as you, but then, you're not going."

"It will take you almost a month to ride to the palace. The princess may be dead before you even arrive."

Robert had a brief vision of his childhood friend being placed in a coffin, her spirit gone forever. "Then I shall leave at first light."

Mr. Vantauge's knuckles gleamed white in the candlelight. "What if you can't save her? People always look for someone to blame. You're placing yourself at the mercy of the king."

"I don't care to impress him. What difference does it make if he blames me?"

"It can make a tremendous difference."

"Look around you." Robert swung an arm at the cabin's cramped interior. His parents' bed stood in one corner, and the family coat of arms, the only visible reminder of their earlier life, hung above the headboard. The cabinet and fireplace rested along the wall at Robert's back, and the loft where he slept stuck out above his head. The entire cabin could have fit within his parents' bedchamber back at the palace. "I doubt the king would bother to follow me here. I don't see him pounding on our door hunting you down."

"No, my brother does it for him through letters." The tone in Mr. Vantauge's voice held a mixture of irony and bitterness. "Even if you succeed in finding the culprit, there is no guarantee he or she will be brought to justice."

"As long as Aurelia is alive, what does it matter?"

"You're a naive fool!"

The argument escalated into a growing spiral, the bedrock of reason crumbling under the scalding flames of emotion.

Robert felt himself wounded time and again by the questioning of his competence, but he fought back with his own unfair accusations, determined not to give ground. The single-minded pressure in his brain propelled him forward. He could not let Aurelia die, not the quick-witted girl who had argued with him in every debate and defeated him in his very first horse race. When he had left the palace it had been with the nagging fear that he might never see her again.

And no matter how much his life had changed, he had never quite managed to shake her from his head. She was always in his thoughts, challenging him to do a better job or goading him to admit when he had made a mistake. She was a constant, unending voice, and he could not accept the thought of her death. He would go to the palace.

"Enough." Mrs. Vantauge's cool voice broke into the flaming atmosphere. "Robert, you know I do not want you to go." She put a hand on her son's shoulder. "I have no more wish to see you place your life in the hands of others than I have to see your father do so in another investigation.

"However." She gave her husband a pleading look. "This is Robert's decision to make. We can't keep him here against his will, Brian. He is old enough to make his own choices."

Mr. Vantauge flung up his hands in disgust and slammed out of the cabin.

Robert winced at the memory. Aurelia's expectant face returned to the forefront of his vision. "My father could not leave the farm," he said in response to her query.

Aurelia nodded, seeming to accept his explanation without question. He supposed the trauma of the recent news had dulled her senses. Instead of prying, she turned a corner.

Palace Hill rose up before them, the steepness of its dramatic slope nothing next to the sheer cliffs hidden on its opposite side. The palace sprawled across the top, a fortress of stone walls embedded in volcanic rock. The tower and turrets, spires and battlements, reached up above the outer wall into the evening sky. A backdrop of gray clouds buried the distant rim of the Valshone Mountains so that only the palace appeared to stand out above the valley floor. Shadows slanted down, masking one side of the ominous structures. A palace built for defense, for intimidation, for deterring the most powerful invading army. The front gate stood open now after a century of peace, but those same doors would slam secure at the first indication of attack.

Secure from an outside threat, but from an inside one? The thought reminded Robert that he did not yet know how Aurelia had managed to enter the city alone. "How did you escape the palace today?" he asked. "After the attack last night, I thought your father had you restricted to your rooms for your own safety."

"Then he ought to have told me the truth." She lifted her chin. "If I tell you how I left, you must swear not to share the information with anyone, not even Chris or your uncle."

His jaw clenched. Uncle Henry had been none too happy about the escapade the night before. On the other hand, if Robert did not learn how she had managed to leave without an escort, how was he to prevent her from doing so in the future? Besides, he had already disobeyed the king's orders by telling her about the assassination plot. What was to prevent her from sharing his secret if he betrayed hers? "I swear."

She ducked under a curtain of willow branches beside the winding road. "I smuggled my way out on a supply wagon. Guards are trained to keep a threat from entering the palace. They rarely inspect wagons going out."

"What about when you return? Won't the guard at the front gate tell your father then?"

"And admit to being on duty when I left?" She popped back out from behind the branches. "No one wants to be that person, Robert."

He tried to squelch a sense of admiration. It took a certain amount of courage, wit, and reckless abandon to manipulate an entire palace guard. Not to mention her father. "Why?" Robert asked. "Drew says you do this often. Why go to all that trouble time and time again?"

She turned around and walked backward up the hill, sweeping a hand at the view below her. "This is my city, Robert, its curves, its hidden crannies. I wanted to know it. Not just the polished mansions and the sculpted gardens, but the warped wooden doors, the rusted balconies, the broken tiles. And the people who live in it. I *do* know them. I can barter with a blacksmith, outsell a paperboy, or coax a tart from a stingy baker."

Or a story from an old seaman, Robert thought.

"I could never do any of those things dressed as a princess," Aurelia said, "with a train of guards at my heels." There was an earnest tone to her voice, an honesty that held him. As did the irony of her words. *That is why the people like her,* he thought. *They want her as a ruler because she does not behave like one.*

As she neared the front gate, Aurelia placed a hand on his shoulder. "Wait awhile before coming through. I would not want the guard to blame you for my leaving."

She began to pull away, but Robert caught her inner elbow. Strands of dark hair had begun to escape from beneath her white cap. "You're safe in the palace where the guards can protect you," he said, willing himself to believe it. "I'm certain that is why the last attempt happened on the street. Tell me you will let me know the next time you leave."

She met his gaze, gave a faint half smile, then removed his fingers from her elbow and walked toward the gate.

The promise did not come.

Chapter Seven
THE PULSE OF POLITICS

The party was lovely, so lovely even Aurelia was enjoying herself. Candles glowed from every windowsill in the ballroom. A mixture of men in dark frock coats and women in blue and purple gowns visited with one another. Champagne glasses clinked, toasting her. Aurelia nodded at the smiling faces, thanking the guests for their good wishes. She stepped through the crowd, steering a path to the dance floor. Someone was waiting for her.

A glimpse of her father brought her to a halt. He was speaking with Henry but turned to salute her with a glass. The king smiled and beckoned. A pathway opened up until she was close enough to hear his voice over the chattering crowd and humming music. He bent his head down close. "I'm so proud of you, my dear," he whispered, giving her a light kiss on the forehead, then raising up in rich laughter. Henry joined in. Aurelia did not catch what they said as she returned to her quest to reach the ballroom's center.

Elise blocked her path, towering oddly above Aurelia's head. The queen's snow-white gown clashed with the sea of dark party wear. She did not look at her stepdaughter, instead resting her eyes above Aurelia's tiara. "Here she is, lost among the crowd," Elise said, her shrill voice echoing above the din. She was speaking to someone just behind Aurelia's left shoulder.

Then she chastised her stepdaughter. "You need to begin the first waltz, silly child. No one can have the pleasure of dancing at your wedding until you do so first." The queen reached out, took Aurelia's hand in her gloved grasp, and pushed with astonishing power.

Stepping back, Aurelia felt a cold, viselike grip close around her upper left arm. It steered her free of the crowd out to the center of the dance floor. The music stopped, and the voices quieted. Even the clinking of crystal ceased. Across the empty space, a thousand eyes blurred into a hazy fog.

The viselike grip on her arm turned her around. She gazed at a black cravat resting on a black silk shirt between the folds of a black frock coat. Her eyes raised to see the face of the owner of the cravat, the shirt, the coat, and the grip molded to her arm. But there was no face to see.

She was staring into the hollow pits of an empty black skull.

Aurelia jolted awake, her chest aching with terror. She gasped for breath, trying to squeeze extra air from the lungs caging her heart. The nightmare skull seared her mind. She reached a shaking hand up to her forehead, pushing back thick strands of hair. Then her eyes ran fearfully around the room, peering into the shadows. Nothing. No one.

She stumbled out of the bed over to the fireplace. Somehow she managed to secure a slender wooden brand and set it on the banked coals. Her trembling fingers took what seemed like hours to transfer the flame to the candle on her bedside table. Finally, light glowed. Her salvation.

A council meeting was called for ten o'clock in the morning. As always, Aurelia was the first to arrive. The room's long mahogany table and matching chairs reflected her father's taste rather than her stepmother's. Perhaps Elise had found the cramped space not worth changing, or perhaps she feared her husband might move the old, sharp-edged furniture elsewhere.

Aurelia slipped into her favorite seat. She could not sit at the table's ends as those were reserved for her father and stepmother, and she would not sit at the back, neither wanting to be trapped nor to give the impression of hiding. She preferred to sit along the outside at least one chair down from her father. This suited her both because it placed her beside Henry, whom she trusted, and because she was close enough to look her father in the eye.

The captain of the guard and the finance minister arrived

next. They scurried behind the table along the wall, burying themselves in the shadows of a thick maroon tapestry. She eyed the captain. The thought of him covering up attempts on her life left a sour film in her throat. Her stomach rolled. Everyone attending this meeting—except her—had probably been aware of the danger.

Henry and the general in charge of the military arrived at the same time, followed by Elise carrying an opal-colored goblet. Thinking everyone except the king had arrived, Aurelia moved to push in two extra chairs on her right.

"Desist!" Chris snatched a chair out of her hand and plopped down on the hard seat. She raised an eyebrow. Henry was always trying to persuade his son to attend meetings in order to "learn through experience," but Chris had not been present for several weeks. She doubted he would ever take over his father's role as king's adviser.

"Thought I'd show Robert how the vital decisions are made." Chris motioned toward the door.

She looked up, stunned to see his cousin slip inside the room. "With royal permission, of course," Robert said.

Elise frowned at Chris, and for a moment Aurelia thought her stepmother might turn Robert away because of his cousin's careless attitude; however, the queen's eyes turned to Henry instead, and the joy on the adviser's face must have convinced her to allow his nephew to stay. She stated smoothly, "You are welcome. There is nothing on today's agenda to exclude the presence of a guest. You are Henry's nephew, I believe?"

"Yes, Your Majesty." Robert gave a slight bow. "Thank you."

She nodded and turned away.

Rather than taking the empty seat beside Chris, Robert slid past Aurelia and his uncle without comment. He pulled out the chair across from Henry and scooted it back from the table, burying himself in the corner by the wall. Aurelia quelled an unwanted wave of distress at having been ignored.

Finally, the king entered the room. His gray head hung low, and his feet shuffled. Everyone stood up at once upon his entrance. He slumped down at the head of the table and began talking before the rest of the council members even had a chance to return to their seats. "I planned to begin this meeting with your usual reports; however, I have just received troubling news from King Edward of Anthone, who is staying with us for a while. He tells me his forces have failed to keep citizens of the Outer Realms from entering his country."

Robert's head jerked up. Aurelia wondered if Robert, too, was thinking of the seaman's story from the day before. It seemed strange that the Outer Realms would become the topic of a council meeting this soon after hearing the tale of the refugee boy.

"A shame." Elise spoke up. "But Edward has never done well protecting his borders. We are fortunate the border we share with Anthone is all desert."

"Still there must be a concern on our part," the general said. "If people from the Outer Realms are smuggling themselves into Anthone, sooner or later they will try to enter Tyralt."

Aurelia thought about the boy in the story. *Why should anyone in need be turned away?*

The king sighed. "Yes, both of you have a point, but you have not listened to the entire issue. My concern is not that a few members of the Outer Realms sneak into Tyralt but that Edward is now lifting his exclusion law."

Aurelia's head snapped up at her father's words. Much as she disliked Edward of Anthone, she found herself trying to squelch a desire to grin. She would have expected the sixty-year-old monarch to be even more obsessed with tradition than her father, but the old scavenger was defying regional policy. That would set every kingdom along the coast up in arms.

"Tell him the change is out of the question," Elise demanded. "We cannot afford to open the gates to the Outer Realms. Think of all the problems which come with refugees. We have enough beggars and thieves on the streets without inviting foreign criminals."

"They wouldn't be criminals, Elise, if we allowed them to enter Tyralt legally," Aurelia argued.

Ignoring his daughter's outburst, the king replied to his wife, "I am afraid telling Edward of Anthone to change his mind is not an option. I asked him to wait to speak with other leaders in the region, but he refused."

Elise raised her voice. "Once again he leaves us to deal with problems he incurs."

"Perhaps it is time to rethink *our* policies," Aurelia said. "Two days ago . . ." She started to tell her father about the protest in the market square.

But Elise interrupted. "The king of Anthone cannot be firm about his decision, my dear," she said to her husband. "After all, he came to you. He must be open to discussing some type of arrangement."

Aurelia eyed her stepmother's goblet, wishing it contained something to induce silence.

The king frowned. "I need time to think about the only request Edward has of me."

A strange hush fell over the room as the listeners waited for details that did not come. Henry tapped his hand softly on the table. "You believe his change in policy is a veiled threat, Your Majesty?"

Aurelia's eyes widened, her brief enthusiasm for Edward's spark of independence snuffed out. She wanted to throttle the man.

"My dear," Elise said to her husband, "the request cannot be that bad. We can't just allow him to disrupt the region. What is—"

"Father, you must reject any request made under intimidation," Aurelia argued.

The queen's gaze settled on her stepdaughter's shoulders. "I shouldn't have to point this out, young lady, but this is not your decision."

"I have as much right to an opinion as you."

Her stepmother's eyes narrowed in icy fury. "The only right you have is to marry someone who will not allow you to destroy this kingdom."

"Do embroider your mouth shut, Elise!"

"Aurelia!" the king boomed, facing his daughter for the first time during the entire meeting. Red lines etched the whites of his eyes, and veins popped out on his forehead.

"Our precious region could do with some disruption," Aurelia continued. "Maybe if we were not enslaved to tradition, Tyralt might actually improve."

"Aurelia . . ." Her father's voice steadied. "It is obvious to me that you have not yet recovered from yesterday's illness. You are excused from the rest of this meeting."

Warning bells went off in her head. If she left, what message would she be sending to the rest of the council? To Elise? She was angry with her father for hiding the truth about the assassination attempts, she realized. He had treated her like a child. Fury wrapped around her brain, and she wanted to scream in outrage.

Her eyes flicked toward Robert. He had been watching the queen, but for a second his gaze met hers with a blue calm. He gave the slightest shake of his head, sending her a message.

She could not attack her father for his secrecy because she had promised to hide her knowledge of the assassination plot. The legs of her chair scraped back across the bare floor, and she left the room, the voice in her head counting and counting and counting to smother her anger.

Robert watched everyone watch her go. A wide smirk stretched across Chris's face. Henry wrinkled his brow in concern. Blank facades hid any emotions felt by the captain, general, and finance minister. The queen took a sip from her goblet and smoothly placed it back on the table. The only person who appeared greatly shaken by the exchange was the king, who leaned back in his chair and closed his eyes.

"I can see I allowed myself to bring this issue to the council without enough thought," he said. "We will cease to discuss it today and progress to other topics." Then he lapsed into silence.

"Perhaps the captain of the guard can share his report," the queen said, rescuing her husband.

The captain began shuffling through papers, and the discussion drifted into a string of reports until the meeting broke up.

"That was the most entertaining council meeting I've ever attended," Chris joked, elbowing Robert in the stomach. "You must be good luck."

"Does the queen always talk that much?"

"Never. Usually the king won't stop. 'Course Aurelia always

has to have her say, just like back when we had class together. She and her father argue sometimes, but I've never seen her take on the queen before."

"The king was certainly upset," Robert commented.

"Yes. Father says the king had a tough time running things after the prince died, but I don't remember His Majesty ever letting someone take over a meeting."

"Do you have any idea what Edward of Anthone wants from him?"

"No, but I'll be certain to tell you as soon as I find out." Chris smiled at the prospect.

"Something was bothering the king."

"Besides the fact that his daughter was almost murdered twice in the last three nights?"

Murdered. Was it any wonder the king had looked on edge? Robert barely lifted a hand as his cousin departed down the hallway. The plot on Aurelia's life had run under the surface of the entire meeting. Robert's sole purpose in attending had been to observe the way the most powerful people in the kingdom reacted to the crown princess. The relationship between the queen and her stepdaughter could certainly be described as explosive.

He set off in search of Aurelia, hoping she had not allowed her anger to propel her too far afield. He tried her rooms first. No one was there except a flustered young lady's maid who could not keep track of her mistress.

Robert headed next to the royal stables. A rare feeling of warmth and peace filled the stables' interior. Wooden boards and beams separated each stall into its own private nook, not only for the horses but for the human visitors as well. One could hang a horseshoe on an outer corner as a signal to the staff and spend hours without interruption. The sight of metal arching over a nail outside his own horse's alcove told Robert he had found Aurelia.

She sat high on the edge of Horizon's stall, her earlier attire exchanged for a unique riding outfit. Its white shirt and brown vest were loose rather than fitted, and tan trousers stuck out from beneath a simple brown skirt. Black riding boots on her feet rested beside a gap in the stall boards.

She was holding out a handful of hay toward Horizon. The stallion snorted, tossing his head and sprinkling Aurelia's hair with fresh green strands.

Robert laughed, moving quickly forward and climbing up on the painted white boards beside her. "He's not impressed with you, Your Highness."

She bent her head toward Robert and shook it, releasing a cloud of hay into his face. "That's only because he has yet to take the time to get to know me." As Robert waved away the cloud, she glared at him. "And it's Aurelia, not Your Highness, to him and to you."

"Aurelia." His voice softened as he reached to remove a final strand of green from behind her ear.

"Ahem." The sound of a man clearing his throat startled Robert into almost toppling from his perch. Drew Fielding, dressed entirely in shiny black satin, stood in the shadow of a tall beam. His black boots rested on the dusty floor and his head remained higher than the heads of both companions perched on the stall boards. White teeth gleamed in a wide grin. "Glad to see you, lad. You're just who we've been waiting to talk with."

Robert struggled to regain his composure. "Have you?"

"Sure. I'm here to collect." Drew stepped forward, holding out a hand to Horizon. "Tell us about this horse. He can't have been bred around here." The stallion sniffed the horseman's fingers and jerked away.

Robert slid a hand over Horizon's cold nose and warm forehead. "No, but his mother was."

"Fantasia!" Aurelia exclaimed, referring to the bay's fine-boned mother. "Father gave her to the Vantauges upon the family's departure from the palace." Pounding on the stall boards in triumph, she turned to Drew. "I told you he was part ours. Look at his head. No wonder it's similar to Bianca's. They both have the same dam."

"Bianca?" Robert inquired, rubbing the smooth black hair on Horizon's forelock.

"My mare," Aurelia said. "She has the same slender head, but she isn't the rebel your fellow is."

"The rebelliousness comes from his father," Robert explained. "My mother nursed a trapper through pneumonia, and he gave us a wild red horse in thanks. The trapper claimed the red was a pure Geordian Desert stallion, won in a gambling match. My father never believed the story. The horse didn't live long, tangled a leg in a barbed-wire fence after siring his only colt.

"Horizon has never been as reckless as his sire," Robert continued, dropping his palm to the stallion's red-brown cheek, then snatching away his hand as the horse snapped sideways with large teeth, "but there are times when I believe he must be descended from desert horses." *The shrill whistle of a challenge when Horizon met another stallion, the ease with which he broke loose from the paddock during a brushfire, the way he ran in the fields without cramping or sweating.* "He's never been exactly tame."

Directing his next words to Drew, Robert said, "I was hoping you could tell me more about him."

"You mean you were hoping I could prove that trapper's story somehow by looking at this horse." Drew chuckled. "Truth is, I can't disprove it, which is saying something. Whoever the sire was, he wasn't bred around the capital. I've heard about the horses in the Geordian, but I don't know what to believe. They're said to be swift, with terrific stamina as well as racing speed. Desert tribesmen don't share their horsemanship outside the region. If this fellow is an example of one of those horses, I may have to plan a trip there myself. He's something. Have you run him on a course?"

Robert shook his head. "I've never raced competitively, and I don't trust him with other riders. He goes well when I need him. I've never been beaten when I wanted to outrun someone."

"I'd like to see him on the palace racecourse," Drew stated, running his hand in a smooth stroke down the stallion's graceful neck. "Just to time you on him at a dead run, no other horses around. Trained jockey or not, it would give us an idea if he's got real racing speed."

Robert shrugged his shoulders. "I don't have time to spend riding around an arena right now."

"Oh, come on, Robert," Aurelia teased. "If you've got time to waste watching a council meeting, you ought to give this fellow a real run." She stretched a hand toward the stallion, and Horizon snorted in her face.

"You only want me to do this because you're a stronger jockey, and you want to embarrass me on the racecourse," Robert accused.

Aurelia plucked a rope halter off the wall and twirled the loose end. "What's the worst that could happen? He could throw you, but with that hard head of yours, you'd be no worse off."

Robert stared her down. "I have other priorities right now. If and when those are resolved, I'll think about your suggestion." The twirling rope came to a halt, and he regretted using the word *if*.

"Speaking of priorities," Drew said, breaking the stillness, "if you'd still like to visit that scarred stallion, I've found a way for you to manage it."

"You have access to Elise's stables?" Aurelia's face lit up. "How are we getting in?"

"Oh no," Robert said, "you're not going. I don't want you near that horse. Plus you'd hardly go unnoticed. A change of clothes won't be enough to keep your identity secret around that place."

She slapped the halter back on its hook and leaped onto the ground. Crossing her arms over her chest, she glared up at Robert. "I suppose I could gain access through the front gate."

"No." He jumped down in front of her. "If you arrive with an entourage, that team of horses might disappear." Her chin jutted, and he could hear air rush into her nostrils; but she did not argue. Robert turned to Drew. "When do we go?"

Wrinkles creased the horseman's forehead, and his eyes ran back and forth between the two young people. "Tonight," he replied.

Chapter Eight

DEPTH

AURELIA MADE HER WAY TOWARD THE LIBRARY AT the back of the palace. She hoped to arm herself with a novel for the coming night's insomnia. It was not fair, she thought, that Robert could go investigate tonight and she was left to battle the terrors of her own imagination. A cold draft gusted down the open hallway, and she wrapped her arms around her chest to stave off the chill. This original section of the palace with its barren walls and ceilings was impossible to keep warm. To her surprise, the library door stood open. No one except her father and her ever came here.

"Father?" Aurelia peered through the door into the dim corner of the library. The patterns of colored glass in the lone window kept out most of the afternoon light. A gray head turned toward the door, then turned back, bending low along an overflowing bookshelf. The figure's weary eyes and strained face muscles did indeed belong to her father.

"Yes." The word came out in a muffled response as he shuffled through layers of sewn book covers.

"I . . . I'm surprised to see you here," she stuttered.

He sighed. "I admit I haven't come here in the last several months. I always know I am in trouble when I am too busy to read."

"I could return later if you would like to be left alone." She edged away, her reason for coming paling beside the memory of the morning's confrontation.

"No." He tugged a thick book from a shelf and straightened to face her. "We should discuss the council meeting."

She lifted her head and stepped forward. "I'm sorry for speaking out of turn, but my opinion is as valid as anyone's."

"Not when you disrespect your stepmother," he answered.

Arguing with him about Elise's merits was fruitless. Aurelia groaned inwardly, sinking into a dark chair with a curved back. The scents of dust and leather clung to the furniture. A silver lamp with a hollow wick sat on the table at her side, and she stared into the glowing glass tube.

Lately she felt as though she could not reach her father, as if an invisible wall stood between them. Perhaps now, without others in the background, she could bring down that wall. She took the opportunity to tell him about the protest in the market two days before. "The guards should be reprimanded," she finished.

"Their rush to action could have sparked injury or even death."

The king set his chosen book down beside the lamp and rubbed his forehead. "The guards may have acted too soon, but they acted on behalf of your welfare. Could you not try to avoid such explosive situations for a while?"

For the first time, Aurelia realized the cause for the guards' overprotective behavior. They had feared another assassination attempt. She blushed, ashamed of not connecting the events earlier. "Do you still intend to enforce the market tax?" she asked. "Or does knowing it will harm the vendors change your mind?"

He sank down in a chair beside hers. "I did not make this choice without thinking it through. The kingdom cannot run without funds, and the sellers in the marketplace gain as much as anyone when people come to town for a royal function."

She had not thought of that. "But what about the people's argument for having a voice in the process? Maybe you could invite a city leader to the palace council meetings."

"I have considered it, Aurelia, but unlike you, I am not anxious to discard years of tradition. Such a change will have results neither you nor I can predict."

"The results might be positive." She stood up. "Besides, Tyralt is changing. With the settling of the frontier and the growing number of schools, the people have more opportunities than in the past. They don't need a lord or a stone wall to protect them from danger. They can make their own decisions and own their own land. They can travel to other parts of the kingdom, and choose their own type of work."

She thought about Robert's parents and how they had given up the ease of palace life to forge their own home. She thought about the hope she had seen on the faces of her former classmates as they scaled the front steps of the university. She thought about her own dreams. And pushed them aside. Her voice was firm. "The council should adapt to those changes."

The king lifted his hand. "When you are queen, you may see that it does."

She hated the idea of her future resting on his death. *How will I know what to do,* she thought, *if you never allow me to make decisions? What if I fail and cannot ask for advice because you are gone?* "I want to help people and effect change now. I'm tired of feeling powerless. Before you became king, didn't it frustrate you to have to wait to have a say?"

"If you want to lead, then you must show the patience required, Aurelia. Being a leader is more about compromise than making choices." He dropped his eyes down to his book.

"Yes, Father." She struggled with what to say next. She wanted to talk to him about the plot on her life, to have him hold her and tell her things would be all right, that he would protect her. Her father—the man who had lost his son and his wife in less than a month; the man who had spent a year in grief, out of reach from even his three-year-old daughter; the man who had married again and started a new life and did not want anything or anyone to interfere with that life. She would find no safety and comfort there. His method of dealing with pain was to pretend it did not exist.

Her gaze drifted to a stack of books on the nearby table. *Relationships of Power, Royal Unions, Marriage Contracts.* In horror, her eyes flew to the leather cover in his hands: *Historical Alliances.* "You're researching my marriage!" she accused.

He looked up from the book, startled. "Would you rather I didn't?" he said. "Would you prefer I toss you out the door with the next man who comes calling, regardless of the impact the union will have? Honestly, Aurelia. You claim you want power, but you refuse to take any responsibility for finding yourself a husband."

She sputtered in anger. "Responsibility? What responsibility? You're going to decide who I should marry."

"Of course. You can't make such a vital decision." His voice deepened. "The future welfare of the kingdom depends on the match you make. You know this, Aurelia. Stop behaving like a child. You've been no help at all. In fact, you seem determined to disrupt the entire process."

"I'm not allowed to decide who I'm to marry, but you think I should support the process?" Her palms clenched into fists. She could feel the heat flaring in her cheeks and her blood pulsing through her veins.

He slammed the book shut. "Yes. Already I've had to explain your behavior to the men you have turned down. Perhaps they were not the best choices, but you might at least have made your refusals seem reluctant. Every time you offend one, you make it harder for me to find a husband for you who can improve the political future of Tyralt."

"Good," she snapped.

His eyes rolled, and he confronted her with the ultimate blow. "You are just like your mother." The statement clung to the air, and she felt the invisible wall spring back up between them.

The Tyralian wall faded in the background as Robert headed west. Drew rode at his side without speaking, leaving the sound of horse hooves to click away the final moments of the dusk. Massive tree trunks lined the northern edge of the Western Road. Slanting branches with shiny green tips crowded the air with the strong scent of fir. On the left, cleared farmland with fields of tiny strawberry plants and thick berry hedges gave way to gentle slopes.

"Remember, lad." Drew broke the silence. "No one comes on Midbury land without an invitation. We're going there at the word of a friend of mine, and far as he knows, we're there to see a colt. Nothing else." The horseman paused, perhaps waiting for Robert to explain the real reason behind the long evening journey, but no such explanation was forthcoming. Drew knew more than enough already.

After more than an hour's travel, the two riders turned north on to a dirt road cutting into the Kryshan Forest. Inky blackness soaked the air, and Robert guided his mount along the road's edge. He had no wish to fall into the path of a carriage along this route. "How far are we from the queen's estate?" he asked as he dodged the threat of a low-hanging branch.

"You're on it, lad. Have been since we turned off the main road. Coming up on the center of the place now." Drew gestured forward.

A thick wall stood amid the trees, its height matching that of the palace's outer wall. This gate was closed, though, and the guard looked stern. Robert was glad to let Drew explain the purpose of their entry. The horseman did not mention the colt, only the name of a friend who was expecting him. The guard grunted and motioned for another man to slip loose the latch and swing open the heavy iron gates. Drew and Robert rode through.

Buildings sprouting chimneys like horns loomed out of the night. Gargoyles seemed to hiss from the eaves of an old manor house, and a new manor towered against clouds of darkness. Ragged tree limbs guarded a tangle of crossing paths, and at the heart of the estate stood the famed Midbury Stables.

After dismounting, Robert tied Horizon to a hitching post. Then he stepped through the wide stable doors and felt his jaw drop. Row upon row of unending stalls stretched out before him, each corridor brilliantly lit despite the late hour. The dirt aisles had been swept clean, and the smell of fresh hay muffled even the scent of manure.

To his right, an open door revealed a tack room the size of a small barn. He drifted toward it, staring in awe at the perfect slanting rows of bridles and halters organized by size. Blankets, cleaned and folded, covered two shelves, and on the remaining shelves sat no fewer than two dozen saddles: every type, every size, every shade. He felt his stomach fall out from under him.

Drew gripped Robert's shirt and tugged, then headed down a long aisle flanked by stalls on either side. "No need to make it obvious you've never been here before," Drew stated. "Stick close. The queen's first husband turned this place into a cursed labyrinth."

"He built it?"

"Designed it. The man was a famous architect, designed projects everywhere, including newer sections of the palace. Made the stables his project after Melony was born. Wanted to stay close to his daughter. Didn't work out, though. Came down with a fever and died only a few months later. The queen watched over the final construction."

A small man sitting on an overturned bucket blocked one side of the aisle. Aged fingers brushed a bridle with a dark cloth. "Hey, Harvey." Drew pulled Robert to a halt beside the man. "Thanks for letting us in to see your new colt."

Harvey looked up from his work, wrinkles splitting into a

wide smile. "What I'd like to know is how you knew that colt was bein' brought in tonight. You're the only bloke I know would travel two hours to get here and two hours back in pitch dark to see a horse."

"I wouldn't bet on that." Drew clapped the older man's shoulder. "I reckon you've done a few crazy things in your life for the love of a horse."

Harvey chuckled. "More than a few, but, seriously, how did you find out about this colt? Edward of Anthone went through a lot of trouble to get him here, and he had us pretty cowed into keepin' mum."

"I was lucky." Drew lifted his hand. "The lad has been pestering me with questions about desert horses. I started doing research, and a fellow down by the docks let slip you lot were collecting a real desert colt this very night. I couldn't turn down the opportunity, and I'm real pleased you allowed Robert to come."

"What Edward don't know won't hurt him." Harvey grinned.

"Speaking of Edward," Robert said, "why is he stabling this colt here instead of at the palace?"

"I suspect it's because desert horses aren't supposed to be bred outside the Geordian," Harvey replied. "Horse breeders been fightin' for years to get rights to Geordian horses, but treaty granted tribes all resources within their territory. Tribes in the Anthone portion give their reignin' monarchs each a horse, but only if all offsprin' are returned to the tribe. I reckon Edward didn't want it whispered about he's broken treaty."

Harvey lowered his voice. "I try to keep my nose out of the politics. We've got horses from every country in the region. A Geordian Desert colt, though, that's somethin' I never thought I'd see in my lifetime."

"Listen, Harvey, I didn't mean to disrupt your work." Drew looked over at Robert. "Seeing as we've got a minute before the colt arrives, I'd like to show the lad around. It's not every day a horseman gets to see a setup the scale of Midbury."

Harvey chuckled. "Show him around. Just act like you belong, and nobody will give you a hard time."

Robert followed Drew past dozens of nickering horses until Harvey's form faded in the background. Then, after turning down a corridor as vast as the first but in this case stabling teams, Drew continued another twenty-five yards and pointed to his left.

Six black horses. Robert picked out the lead stallion right away, and it picked him out as well. None of the other horses in the stables had responded to his presence with more than an outstretched neck; but this stallion snorted, shook his head, and raced to the back of his stall.

"Not too fond of visitors, that one," Drew said.

A chill tingled Robert's jaw. Wild eyes rolled in his direction. The black head lifted; neck muscles strained. The stallion rushed the boards, lifting his deep chest and pounding the rattling wood with the same powerful forelegs that had haunted Robert's dreams. Dust billowed from the stall door, and thudding echoed down the walkway, drawing the attention of stable hands.

Robert backed away, pulling Drew with him clear around the corner.

"Myself, now," teased Drew, "I'd pick about any other horse in this stable for laying down my money." Robert ignored the comment. In the back of his mind, he had not really believed the horses would be here, not the same team from Carnival night, not that scarred stallion. "That was him?" prompted the horseman.

Robert nodded, reality sinking in. "Is there a way to find out who drove him two nights ago?"

"You could try asking. There aren't many drivers could handle a team like that."

Something in Drew's tone made Robert look up at his companion. "You know who drives that team," he accused.

The horseman hesitated. "I know a fellow who has driven that team. I can't be certain he was driving it the night you saw him." A pause. "Harvey ought to be able to tell you. He sees everything."

Robert retraced his steps. With the name of the driver, he

would have the name of the assassin—at least one assassin.

Harvey still sat on his bucket in the aisle, his fingers caressing another bridle. "Enjoy your trip, youngin'?"

"He was enjoying it up until we ran into that mean black stallion of yours," Drew answered. "What's his name again?"

"Animosity." Harvey frowned. "Stupid name for a horse."

"Seems a handful," said Drew, propping a foot on a grain sack. "I've never seen anybody but Gregory take that horse out."

"No one else can handle him." A bitter scent of polish wafted through the air as Harvey shook out his rag.

Plunging into the conversation, Robert said, "I thought I saw that team with the stallion a couple nights ago."

Harvey nodded. "Gregory had them saddled up late, night of Carnival."

Gregory, Gregory, Gregory—the assassin's name pulsed in Robert's thoughts. No longer just a driver, but a man with a name. "Where was he headed?"

"It's here!" A distant shout interrupted the conversation before Harvey could answer. "Over in the east corral." A crowd of people poured into the corridor from around corners, out of stalls, through doorways; the stables suddenly teamed with men, women, and children. Robert felt himself scooped up and swept down the aisle, Drew and Harvey with him.

"Where are all these people coming from?" Robert called, his feet struggling to keep pace with the crowd as he turned one corner, then another.

"All over Midbury," Harvey answered. "This place is stocked with underground tunnels." He gestured to the right, where a row of seven or eight doors lined a wall. "Each of these doors leads somewhere. That one there will take you a couple miles east of here into the woods. In case you ever want to walk two miles in the dark."

Robert did not have time to consider the chilling prospect as the crush of the crowd shoved him up against the smooth planks of a corral. A golden head tossed in the corral's center. Dark halter straps gleamed on the colt's face, and a lead rope whipped about like wet cloth.

"He's of racing age," Drew crowed.

The colt bolted from its stance, galloped in a broad circle, and reared up, a blazing sun burning in the dark. Shoulder muscles gleamed above a smooth back and powerful hindquarters. Eyes snapped with fear, and the lead rope dangled dangerously. Robert fought a sudden urge to tear the crowd away.

Motioning toward a lone man perched on top of the corral's far side, Harvey said, "Speakin' of Marcus Gregory."

The assassin. From this distance, Robert could not make out facial features, but he took in the slicked hair, long arms, slim torso, and short legs. Perhaps a couple inches over five feet, the man could not weigh more than 110 pounds—the unmistakable build of a jockey.

Robert's assessment was confirmed immediately. Gregory hurtled into the paddock, snatched up the loose lead rope, and sprang onto the colt's back. Twisting in terror, the horse tried to unseat its invader, but Gregory gripped the golden belly with strong legs. Arm muscles bulged as he clutched the horse's mane. The rope flashed into motion, beating the colt about the head until blood dripped from its ear.

Instinctively Robert lurched forward, longing to rip the bully from the horse's back. Drew's strong grip pushed down on Robert's shoulder. "You can't go in there, lad," Drew said. "Turn around, and walk back to the stables."

Robert fled, unable to shake the vision of blood from his thoughts. The faint sound of Drew's voice apologizing to Harvey ebbed in the background. Robert moved without seeing, down the corridor, around the corner, down another corridor, around another corner, on and on. A net of dripping red draped over his mind, interfering with his ability to discriminate. He could not tell one stall from the next, much less one row or one intersection. Winding walls and empty halls closed in on him. The farther he ran, the tighter they gripped him, until the stalls were gone, the hay, the pitchforks, the light.

Emotionally drained, he leaned his body up against a beam and waited for his eyes to adjust to the sudden dimness. He must have left the stables altogether. Instead of stalls, a solid wall rose up before him, featuring doors and windows with bars. He eased away from the beam to peer into one of the windows.

The noxious smell of urine and molding hay boiled his tender insides. Stomach muscles heaved, emptying their contents onto the dirt floor. Gagging, he pressed the palm of his hand to his chest, then slid the hand up to cover his mouth and nose. His eyes strained against the shadows. He could just make out a set of metal chains anchored along the far wall. A dungeon, probably long out of use, but still reeking.

He turned around to backtrack, more anxious than ever to remove himself from his surroundings. *Just get out,* he told himself. *Once you get out of this building, you can walk around the outside and find Horizon. Drew will meet you there.* Embarrassed by the blind flight, Robert moved back into the stables and turned down a corridor. *Keep moving in this direction. Sooner or later, you'll hit the outside wall or an exit.*

Sure enough, in less than ten minutes, he stepped into open air. His lungs expanded with relief... and caught.

Not five yards from the stable entrance sat a black carriage, its sleek sides and plain trim blending into the darkness. The carriage from Carnival night. And out the carriage door stepped Edward, king of Anthone.

Chapter Nine
COURTING DANGER

THE VANTAUGE COAT OF ARMS ON THE SITTING-room wall seemed to gaze at Robert with disappointment. He slumped into his uncle's chair. A full week had passed since the trip to Midbury, and he was no closer to solving the case than he had been the night Edward stepped out of that black carriage.

Perhaps King Edward was not involved in the plot at all. Perhaps he was here solely on a diplomatic mission; but as each day passed, Robert found that less and less likely. The Anthonian king showed no sign of returning to his own country, no sign of cooperating with Aurelia's father, no sign of enjoying Tyralt. Day after day, he met in King Lauzon's official chamber, yet nothing ever seemed to come from the meetings.

Aurelia might know more, but a lot of good that would do Robert. He ran his hands through the waves of his hair in frustration. Here was the crux of the problem. For a week he had been trying to make contact with the crown princess to no avail. He could not find her alone, and the notes he had left with her lady's maid never came back with a reply. Thinking someone might be screening his messages, he had even sent Chris to deliver a note in his stead. There had been no response.

"Any luck with Her Royal Highness?" Chris poked his head in the doorway. "I hear she's going to be stuck in the throne room all day."

"Not unless you consider silence to be fortunate."

Chris walked in, lifted the strap of his scabbard over his head, and propped his sword against the wall. "Anything else I can help you with?" he asked.

"Have you ever heard of a man named Marcus Gregory?"

"Marc Gregory?"

"Marcus, yes. He works as a driver for the queen's stables, and I'm certain he's a jockey as well."

A baffled look crossed Chris's face. "You know how much attention I pay to horses, Rob. I can ask my father. He never has a spare minute, but I can always conjure up a way to get into trouble. That should garner his attention."

"Don't bother. I already asked him. Besides, he's helping the king hammer away at Edward of Anthone again."

Chris propped a foot on the bottom rung of a stool. "I think they ought to just send the old vulture back to his kingdom before Edward rips into any more Tyralian policy."

"He may be doing a lot worse than ripping into policy." Robert stood up and crossed to the other side of the room near the coat of arms. The large shield with its symbol of gold bars supporting the crown mocked him. What had made him think he could continue the family tradition? He turned so that the shield was at his back.

His cousin's eyes were wide. "You think Edward is behind the assassination plot?"

Robert opened his mouth to explain, then shut it. His father's words crept into his thoughts. *Never make an accusation until all the pieces fall into place.* "Listen, Chris, I really need to know what Edward wants from the king."

"I can try again, but I must have asked that question five times last week after the council meeting. Father says it's none of my affair."

Ahhhhh! Robert whirled and slammed his hand against the wall. The coat of arms slid from its hook, banged into the desk below, and crashed to the ground. As the clang echoed throughout the room, both cousins stared down at the damaged metal. A deep dent marred the shield's central symbol.

"I'll see what I can find out," Chris said, bolting for the door.

Robert slouched against the wall, his knee and forehead pressed to the bare surface. His slip of the tongue just now about King Edward reminded Robert he had to be careful about sharing his suspicions.

Who could he trust? He had a sinking feeling he knew why

his father had needed to escape this job. Who was likely to plot against a member of the royal family? People of high rank. People Robert could not afford to cross without consequences. The queen. The king of the neighboring kingdom. And all the people under them.

Add to this the fact that Robert could not share his fears with Aurelia's father without evidence, and almost everyone became an unsafe haven for information. Uncle Henry wanted Aurelia alive, yes, but he worked for the king first. And Robert could not ask Chris to withhold information from his father. Not that Chris would have minded, but with a father like Uncle Henry, planning to keep a secret and doing so were two different things.

But keeping Chris out of the loop created a gaping hole in Robert's resources. Chris had the contacts and the current knowledge about court life. Without Chris, Robert needed help. Someone inside the palace. Someone he could rely on. Someone with the same knowledge as his cousin. Apart from Chris, only one person fit that role.

Robert straightened. He could not wait any longer. If Aurelia was in the throne room today, then that was where he would talk to her.

Aurelia felt Robert grab her elbow. She flinched, not used to having anyone touch her when she was dressed for court. The guards in the throne room doorway leaped forward, and in her surprise, she barely remembered to wave them off.

"I need to talk with you," said Robert.

"Let me go," she snapped. "This room has a thousand eyes." For days she had been waiting for him to tell her about his trip to Midbury, and she had not seen him once. If her father had not demanded her presence today, she would have sneaked off for the haven of the city streets—alone, since her escort was no longer worried enough to make himself available.

She tugged away. For someone who was trying to protect her, he little realized the danger he was courting. Throne-room gossip was a weapon more destructive than cannon. Even now she could feel her stepmother's poison stare boring into her forehead.

The attempt to salvage his reputation was wasted. As she continued toward her place at the left front corner of the room, he grabbed her elbow again. "Today, Aurelia. I need to speak with you today. I've sent several messages in the past week, but you haven't responded."

She frowned. "I have to spend the entire day at court. The earliest I can see you will be after supper." Her voice hardened. "Now please remove your hand from my arm."

Anger flushed his face, but she didn't recognize the cause until she had already swept down the aisle and taken a seat. Of course he was angry. He thought she had refused to answer his messages—but she had never received any. Was someone keeping him from helping her? That seemed impossible. The only people who knew why he was there were her father, Henry, and Chris. They would not keep him away.

Who else had the power to screen her messages? Her gaze dived upon Elise. The queen sat on the dais beside her husband with the same stiff and powdered bearing she always wore at court, a frozen expression for each petitioner and honored guest.

Anger swelled in Aurelia, expanding as the morning progressed. The heat of an uncommonly beautiful day radiated through the arched windows and seeped into every corner of the throne room. It spared no one: not the petitioners huddling at the back, not the courtiers lining the aisle, not the king and queen sitting at the front, and not the princesses watching in their gilt chairs on opposite sides of the room. Beads of sweat lined Aurelia's neckline and tickled the small of her back. Warmth drenched her petticoat and court gown, and her mind stretched for an escape.

From her spot between the king and the courtiers, she could see everyone and everything: the gold patterns on the side of her father's throne, the flicking fans of bored audience members, and the sullen look on Robert's face as he slumped in a chair by the doorway. He looked utterly frustrated, yet there he was, still waiting, despite the fact that she had dismissed him when he had approached her. It was a maddening trait of his, this undeniable patience. The only way past it was to give him what he wanted.

Salvation slid into her mind. Her back straightened, her shoulders squared, and her head lifted. Robert's stubbornness could be just as powerful as hers. Why not give him what he wanted and fulfill her own desires at the same time? If he was brave enough to take a risk.

She made a quick motion for a servant boy to approach. "I need a pen and several pieces of paper," she whispered. Within moments, the boy had returned with a quill pen, an ink bottle, and three sheets of stiff parchment.

On the first sheet, Aurelia scribbled a message to the kitchen staff. On the second, she wrote to the stables. The third was for Robert.

Mr. Vantauge, if you wish to complete your plans today, you must present yourself to my father before court is dismissed for the noon hour. Request his permission for me to attend you on a picnic outing. My father must be informed before I may be granted leave to depart.

She did not bother to sign the message. It was not as if anyone in the room would fail to notice she had passed it to Robert. Her stomach turned at the thought. But he had already ignored the threat of court gossip once this morning. Perhaps he would do so again. Craning her neck to check for his presence, she lifted the note and passed it to the servant.

Robert took the parchment from the boy's hands rapidly, as
if he had expected it and was wondering why it had taken her
this long to respond to his demand. He bowed his head over
the words, then met her eyes with a look of appalled shock. She
could see the thoughts whirling in his mind: *A picnic? And
present himself to her father? In court!*

Her gaze held steady. His dropped to the intimidating aisle
lined by courtiers waiting for a victim to distract them from
their corseted cages. Robert stood up, and for a moment she
thought he might walk out, rejecting her dare and leaving her
behind to simmer for the rest of the day.

But instead he moved toward the man who was listing those
who wished to speak with the king. Robert's name would be
placed at the top, considering his uncle's position. Within minutes the announcer's voice rang throughout the room. "May it
please Your Majesty, Robert Vantauge."

A strange skittering ran through Aurelia's veins, not the triumph she had expected to feel, but something else, as if it were
her own heart on the line, moving up the aisle in front of the
critical whispers and skeptical gazes.

But Robert did not waver. For the first time all morning, he
looked neither uncomfortable nor out of place. His borrowed
court clothes fit as though he had been born to them, and he
held his head erect as he stepped up to the platform. His eyes
met the king's gaze with confidence. *As if speaking with my
father were perfectly natural.*

Aurelia missed the brief exchange of greetings, her thoughts tangled with emotion. She had to remind herself this was only a dare.

"Your Majesty," Robert said without hesitation, "I would like your permission to take your daughter on a picnic." Nothing improper, nothing fancy, every word stated without a glint of anxiety.

Then why do I feel nervous?

"Well, young man." Her father chuckled. "Far be it from me to grant or deny my daughter an opportunity. You may address the Princess Melony with your plans and proceed as she sees fit."

Aurelia's heart plummeted. Of course the king would assume Robert was asking for Melony. Melony's suitors begged the king for scraps of his daughter's time. Suitors for Aurelia brought bribes and mediators. She was not desirable or even pretty. She was only a means to political advancement.

Robert did not allow the error to affect his demeanor. Instead, he complimented her father. "It is my honor to have a ruler who values the rights of his citizens and family members."

"I have raised my children to make wise choices," said the king, nodding with pride.

Within the limits of your parameters.

"I am afraid my request was unclear," Robert continued, returning to the main point of the conversation. "I had meant to ask to spend the afternoon with my former classmate, Princess Aurelia. I understand her presence here is important, and I would not deprive you of her company if it causes difficulty."

Her heart scaled back up her rib cage and kept on soaring. Robert had done it. Asked to court her in public. And what could her father do? He had been praised for valuing his daughters' freedom and had been all too willing to accept the praise.

"Yes, um, well . . . ," stumbled the king, then managed a shaky, "my reply stands. You may ask the lady in question."

Robert nodded as though he had expected this all along. Aurelia reined in the desire to applaud. She held herself still, waiting for him to turn around and walk back down the aisle. Once a suitor obtained her father's permission, the suitor must present his request to the princess either through a written note or a private audience.

Robert, however, did not retreat down the aisle. Instead he turned to face her, strode forward, and swept her a deep bow. "What say you, Your Highness?" His voice carried throughout the room. "Will you come with me this afternoon?"

Her breath left her as his eyes drilled into hers. For a moment she forgot she had pushed him into this, that this had been her idea instead of his and that he was standing there at *her* request. Her whole body tingled at the boldness of his action.

Then she realized this was his revenge. He was daring her to put her own reputation on the line. Air whooshed back into her lungs, and she matched him stare for stare. "I would be honored."

Publicly escorting the crown princess proved a less than private honor. Robert needed only one look around the earthen courtyard to realize his folly. Dressed in her riding clothes, Aurelia stood beside a beautiful gray mare. The young lady's maid stood at her mistress's elbow. And more than ten mounted guards lined the front gate, their saddles bristling with weaponry. *Wonderful.*

He should have known better. *Aurelia* should have known better. Too late now to escape back to Uncle Henry's rooms, Robert glared at her and climbed onto his stallion. He had given up his anonymous standing at court for the chance to talk with her in private, and now he would be lucky to ever have a moment alone with her again.

With no sign of regret, she swung onto the mare and called for a groom to bring up the mount for her lady's maid. The groom bowed, stepped back, and came forward with a huge beige stallion. Robert struggled not to laugh. The horse towered higher than Horizon and must have weighed forty pounds more—a warhorse, perhaps even a charger.

The young girl took one look up at the stallion's empty saddle and backed away. "I... I don't think I can... that is... I am afraid I do not know how to ride, Your Highness. Perhaps I can find you another chaperone." The girl bowed her head in shame. "I... I'm terribly sorry."

Aurelia tossed her head. "Nonsense, Minuet. I'm certain the guards can serve as my chaperones. Do not give it another thought. Let's go, Bianca." The gray mare broke into a walk before the lady's maid even had a chance to respond.

Robert pulled up alongside the princess. "Nicely done," he murmured under his breath, "but I doubt a dozen guards will be as easy to dispose of."

She ignored him, instead flashing a dazzling smile toward Filbert, who sat mounted at the front of the line. "We're headed out along the Western Road. Lead the way, Corporal."

A barrier of armed men and horseflesh blocked Robert's view all the way through the city and out onto the Western Road. Horizon, who was no happier than his rider with the close escort, spent the entire journey straining at the bit and shuffling his hooves. By the time a road going south appeared, Robert was ready to throttle his horse, not to mention Aurelia, for getting him into this mess.

She ordered the guards to stop. "Wait here," she told Robert, then rode up toward the front of the line. He took the moment to regain his bearings. The Kryshan Forest to his right seemed to go on forever. On his left, a field of thick berry hedges ended at the crossroads. A stand of birches lined the road's western edge, and a post painted with the royal crest rose up beside the trees. *This must be the entrance to the extended palace grounds,* Robert thought.

Moments later a shout came back through the ranks. "Dismount!" The guards at his side swung down from their horses.

Aurelia cantered close and motioned Robert onto the southern path. He followed her over a small hill and down through a shallow dip, out of sight from the main road. "That was a hideous experience," he said as soon as the guards could no longer hear him. "What did you say to dismiss them?"

"I told Filbert if he and his men waited at the crossroads, we would meet them there later." She stretched out a hand and let it glance off the white bark of several trees.

"And he agreed to that?"

"Not at first, but he did after I reminded him who let us out the gate on Carnival night."

"You threatened to tell your father?"

"I didn't, and I wouldn't. But if Filbert thinks I would, he deserves to wait at those crossroads." She encouraged the mare to pick up her pace.

Robert pulled Horizon to a halt. "Maybe we should go back. Remember what happened the last time we took advantage of Filbert."

Aurelia reined in Bianca. "You're the one who demanded I talk with you. Don't tell me now that it wasn't important."

"It is, but I assumed we'd talk at the palace. If someone comes after you here . . ." He peered warily through the birches. The trunks stood well apart from one another, light streaming through the gaps.

"Look, Robert, I did not go to all this trouble to spend a gorgeous day like today inside. No one knows where we're going except me, so unless you're the one trying to kill me, we should be perfectly safe." Her shoulders rose and fell as she took a deep breath. "Besides, the palace may not be the best place to talk. I think Elise has been screening your messages. I did not receive any of them."

His eyebrows lifted. The queen could certainly order any servant in the palace, not to mention Aurelia's young lady's maid, to hand over Robert's correspondence. "Do you think the queen is trying to interfere with my investigation?"

"She doesn't know why you're here."

"She might. We don't know what the king has told her."

"Whatever her role, I'm not going to allow her to stop us from talking." Aurelia urged Bianca forward.

The gray mare stepped with ease onto a narrow dirt trail, and Horizon followed in her footsteps through the sunny stand of white birch, across a speckled meadow of gold and green, and over a sloping hill. At the foot of the hill, a slender creek burbled its way over shiny stones. Aurelia turned her mount upstream.

Within minutes they came to a grassy incline with a thin white waterfall springing over a series of jutting crags. Whistling voices of birds challenged the water's rippling song, and the pure scent of wildflowers drifted about the stream. A wide, flat rock rested halfway up the slope, water pouring over one end. Most of the gray slab stretched out dry in the sun. Aurelia swung down and moved to unpack the picnic lunch onto the dry granite.

"Have I been here before?" Robert asked.

"Maybe. I used to come here with friends." She laid out two cloth napkins, several glass jars filled with preserves, and a round tin. "There are easier spots to reach, but I have always liked this one."

"Why is that?" He unlatched the strap around Horizon's girth.

"When I was little, Daria's father told me Jimmy used to race horses on the meadow near here."

The name sounded familiar, but Robert could not place it. "Jimmy?"

"I always called my older brother Jimmy. He preferred it to James. I started coming here because it made me feel closer to him. Other people come in the summer sometimes, but I've never seen anyone this time of year."

Uncertain how to respond, Robert moved toward her mount. Though of course he had known about her brother's death, he could not remember ever hearing her talk about her elder sibling before. Unhooking the saddle, the one that had been repaired without Aurelia's knowledge, Robert inspected the fine leather, testing its strength in his hands. The stitches remained taut. Any clues had been erased by the strap's repair.

He slumped down on the warm granite beside Aurelia, and soon they both indulged in biscuits slathered with rich toppings; the sweetness of strawberry jam melded with honey butter. Between bites, he shared what he had learned during his trip to Midbury.

She listened without flinching. "Did Harvey ever tell you why Gregory took the team Carnival night?"

"No, but he told Drew, who told me. Gregory was assigned to drive Edward of Anthone."

The biscuit in her hand froze on its way to her mouth.

"Edward arrived in Tyralt on Carnival night," Robert continued to explain. "Gregory picked him up from the port and brought him to the palace."

"Do you think Edward was in the carriage when it came after us?"

"There's no way of knowing." Robert wiped a sticky hand on a napkin and told her about Edward's colt.

Aurelia frowned at the description of the golden horse. "If the colt is wild, I suppose my father might be the one who wanted it stabled at Midbury instead of the palace. He has never been easy around horses—not since Jimmy's death."

Jimmy's death. Another voluntary reference to what had always been a taboo subject. Robert dared to pursue the topic. "Why not?"

"He still feels guilty." Her voice was soft.

Robert struggled for a response, not wanting to admit his confusion.

It must have been apparent, though, because she continued: "You know how my brother died?"

"Yes." He had heard reports, though he could not say he actually remembered learning of the incident. At the time,

Robert had been quite young and had not yet known Aurelia. "His horse spooked at a snake and threw him during a hunting expedition."

She shook her head, her face unreadable. "That's the public version of the story. He *was* thrown—right in front of my father. But Jimmy didn't die from the fall. He was trampled by my father's horse."

Aurelia leaned back until her elbows rested on stone. She breathed for a moment, then whispered, "When he died, this central pillar holding everything up disintegrated. Since then my father has been busy trying to build up all the pieces around it. Except there's still no center, so the structure is never stable. Father keeps trying and trying, but he can't get around that fact. I'm not sure which one of us misses Jimmy more."

Robert stayed silent, not wanting to break the spell. She had never let him into her personal life before. Maybe that night on the bridge, but no—that night he had done all the sharing, about his life and his dreams. She had sidestepped his question about her schooling and exploded when he asked why she did not travel. He had wondered about her reaction at the time but failed to pursue it. Only now was he beginning to see what a mess she was inside.

After a long pause, she continued: "I can't help but feel if my brother were here it would solve all my problems. I'm sure my father feels the same way."

"Then you are both wrong." Robert ran his thumb along a

narrow crevice in the rock. "How can you know what life would have been like? Your problems would be different, but they would still exist."

A sigh escaped her throat. "I know that in my head, but my heart isn't easy to convince."

As grateful as Robert was to have earned her trust, he knew his insight was not what she needed. "Maybe you should talk with your father about how you feel."

She shook her head. "I've tried dozens of times. He has too much to worry about without my concerns. He lives like somebody walking on a glass chessboard. The surface looks good, but the slightest crack might send him crashing through the squares. The older I get, the less he wants to talk to me."

"Why?" asked Robert, striving to understand.

Wrinkles furrowed her smooth brow. "I think I remind him of my mother. I look like her. After she left the palace, he destroyed most of her pictures, but I still have a small portrait about the size of your palm. She was plain like me."

What? Robert stared in disbelief. The young woman beside him with her honey-brown skin and the sun glinting off her face was so far from plain that he would have accused her of flirting if it weren't for the sincere tone in her voice. He opened his mouth to argue, then thought better of it. If he told her how she looked to him, there would be little to keep him from confessing the way she made him feel, and this was not the time. Not when she was clearly hurting and in need of someone in whom to confide. Instead he asked a question he had always wondered about. "Why did your mother leave?"

"You mean why did she abandon my father and me after Jimmy's death? Father won't say. Maybe it's my fault." The raw pain on Aurelia's face made Robert wish he had not asked.

He had always prided himself on seeing beyond Aurelia's status to the real person underneath, but it had never occurred to him that she might not see her own strengths, that her sharp tongue and strong opinions might hide a foundation of self-doubt. Had she let her father's grief mar her own sense of worth? And had she given up her own dreams, not because she wanted to rule the kingdom but because she felt it was her duty, her only means of earning her father's love?

"Talking with friends has always been easier than talking with my father," Aurelia added, then paused. "It is nice to have someone who still treats me as a friend."

"What do you mean?" Robert scrambled to keep up with the twist in her commentary. "You've always had friends."

"They've changed around me, the friends we used to have in class. They aren't comfortable with the attention." She began fumbling around, picking up the lunch materials. "Like you on the ride here, having to follow all those guards." She stood up. "I could see your mind turning, thinking you were trapped and wanting to get away."

He started to interrupt, but she overrode him. "Oh, my old friends haven't been cruel. I know it's not about me, but one by one they drifted away. Daria was the last."

He saw, then, what these last few years must have been like for her, watching her classmates go on to their own pursuits while she remained behind. And even worse, having them abandon her friendship because it was too hard.

"What about Chris?" Robert took the napkins and jars from Aurelia's hands and slid the items under the basket lid. "He's still in the palace."

"Chris?" A threat of humor tinged her voice. She backed off the rock and onto the grassy hillside. "He and I have never been close. He's only spending time with me because you're here, Robert. Even you," she said, looking away, "you're only here because of your job."

Something inside Robert snapped. Now she was lumping him in with all the people who had let her down, reducing his relationship with her to no more than duty. He could not let her do that, could not allow her to see him through that warped lens. He moved forward and gripped her shoulders. "Never." His voice was harsh. "Never think that!" He backed away, surprised at the strength of his reaction. Yelling at her would scarcely help.

Her eyes widened.

Embarrassed, he looked down, unable to avoid the tremble in his voice. He could not bear it if she were afraid of him. He had to correct this, now, even if it meant crossing a line. "I . . . I would not be here if I didn't consider you my friend." *More than a friend.* "Do you think I would have traveled this far to help your father . . . or your sister?"

She stayed silent.

Coward, he thought. *Look at her.* He lifted his head and instantly regretted the action. Salt water veiled her eyes, and in that moment he would have done anything to remove those tears.

"I . . . ," she managed to whisper. "I thought you came because your uncle asked you."

"He asked my father," Robert corrected in a soft voice and stepped forward, unable to leave her standing there alone. "I am here"—his hands slid back up to her shoulders, this time very gently—"because of you." He could not help himself. His lips came down to hers, telling her as tenderly as possible why he had come.

Chapter Ten
INTENSITY

AURELIA COULD NOT BREATHE. OR THINK. THIS WAS not—she had not expected this. Her heart pounded in her ears as Robert drew back in slow motion. She avoided his gaze, unable to deal with the emotions swarming over her chest, her brain, her hands. Heat and loss, joy and fear, desire and embarrassment.

Her eyes landed on her horse. Motivated by a terrible instinct to run away, she headed for Bianca. A coat of warm gray horsehair restrained the panic. Aurelia swung onto the bare back and dug her heels into the mare's sides.

But Robert stepped forward, blocking her path. His hands hung loose, and she did not dare look at his face. He must be standing there to apologize, to say he was sorry—that he had not meant it. And she could not, she *could not* listen to him say it, because somewhere deep down under all her chaos and confusion, she hoped he had.

As if controlled by another source, she urged Bianca around him into a gallop, calling in a foreign voice, "I'll race you on the meadow. Show me what that stallion of yours can really do!"

And she was gone, down the creek bed, over the hill, onto the meadow. She cantered Bianca in a large circle. A spotted thrush burst from the brush, its harsh call scolding her for disturbing its hiding place. *Coward, coward, coward,* her mind thumped to the sound of Bianca's even strides. How could she have been so rude? Why couldn't she have just blushed and turned away? What if he didn't come after her?

Horror. She was going to have to return. The picnic basket and the saddle were there.

He might think she wanted him to go away.

He might leave her behind.

He might—

The rhythmic sound of cantering hooves broke into her thoughts. Two saddles and the picnic basket tumbled to the ground. Hooves sped to a gallop. Robert's hair streamed away from his face, and she heard him shout, "Come on!" as he swept past her.

The race. She whirled Bianca, heels digging into the mare's sides. The gray horse gathered speed, her smooth gait seeming to skim over the earthen surface. Air blasted Aurelia's ears, blocking other sound with the power of its roar. Speckled meadow grasses blurred into obscurity. Moving muscles propelled her forward, and she felt . . .

Free. Freedom must feel like this; the air, the space, the absolute absence of control. Time had suspended itself beneath the pounding hooves. She gave herself up to it, burying her head against Bianca's neck and letting herself enjoy the moments of thoughtless flight.

Three quarters of the way across the meadow, she looked up to see Robert circling his stallion into a loop all the way on the other side. She gasped and pulled up in astonishment, her pulse throbbing as her lungs sucked in fresh meadow air. Bianca fought the bit, and Aurelia patted the sleek gray neck. "That's all right, Bianca." She turned the mare toward the hill where Robert had dropped the saddles. "No one ever trounced us like that before."

As she approached the slope, Horizon's familiar snout drew up on her right side. Aurelia eyed the large stallion. His coat gleamed more red than brown in the bright sunlight, and he lifted his neck and tail with pride. *Braggart,* she thought, *but you deserve it.* Despite the race, Horizon's breathing remained as relaxed as earlier that day. "He may not have the papers to prove it," she said, "but he certainly runs like a desert horse. Bianca and I may need a week to regain our overconfidence."

Robert smiled and swung off the stallion's back. "Would you like to ride him?" he asked.

The gesture even more than the opportunity took Aurelia

by surprise. She had seen the way Robert treated his horse, with humor and strength and always a great deal of respect. He would not make the offer to just anyone. For the second time that day, he had left her speechless.

Unable to voice her thoughts, she dismounted and let herself study the magnificent stallion as Robert went about replacing the blanket and saddle. Horizon's broad chest loomed at the height of her shoulders, and his ears flicked sideways as if to tell her she had no business trying to ride him. *That is what you think.* She gathered her patience, knowing this would be no ordinary ride.

Then, taking the reins into her left hand, she mounted. Horizon froze: elbows and knees locked into place. He was testing her, waiting for her to make a mistake. One step at a time, then, no rushing ahead of herself. She patted him on the neck, and politely asked him to go.

No response.

She tried again, this time changing her tone to a command.

No response.

At her side came the sound of Robert smothering a laugh, but she kept her focus on the animal below her. Holding her temper in check, she allowed her brain to click away at the problem. The stallion wanted her to dislike him, wanted her to give up and choose a simpler mount. But it was the challenge that appealed to her, that and his speed. She kicked with her heels and applied a slight pressure to his belly. Then more pressure. And more.

Horizon stood like a mausoleum.

"Robert, hand me my whip," she said, speaking for the first time since mounting. Robert creased his forehead and bit his lower lip as if trying not to refuse.

"Don't look at me like that," she said, taking the short leather instrument from him. "I'm not going to harm your precious stallion. The worst that can happen is he'll punish me."

Exactly, Robert's face seemed to say.

The whip hit the dark rump, and Horizon bolted. Aurelia curled around his long neck, securing her grasp and letting the crop spiral to the ground as she hung on. Horizon lurched in one direction, then another, trying to hurl her off. He bucked. He reared. He raced across the meadow in a zigzagging dance of circles and lines, starts and stops. The soft earth churned under his sharp hooves and pounding hindquarters.

Aurelia waited—a still, clinging body on the horse's back. She could not win this fight with logic or knowledge, only with patience. But when it came to animals, she had patience. With Horizon, she could afford to wait. She waited until his sides heaved in huge panting breaths. Sweat gleamed on the brown-red coat, and his head drooped from exhaustion.

Then she eased her chest up off the stallion's neck and began putting him through his paces. Horizon went left when she said left. He went right when she said right. He trotted, cantered, and even leaped over a fallen tree trunk at the meadow's edge.

"And how, madam, am I going to make it back to the palace

on this pitiful excuse for a horse?" teased Robert when she finally dismounted.

Removing the saddle from the stallion's back, she plopped down on the ground. "I guess you'll have to stomach my company while he recovers." Dropping onto her back, she rested a hand on her forehead. It came away shining with sweat. Her hair blew out in a halo of loose strands around her face, and she tossed the remaining hairpins into the grass. Then propping herself up on her elbow, she looked at Robert.

Worry shadowed his face as he traced a design on the back of Bianca's saddle. *He does nothing but worry,* she thought. *Worry about talking to me, worry about not talking to me.* "Tell me about training horses on the frontier," she said.

His face cleared. Its lines and hollows began to shift with animation, and the tone of his voice rose and fell with expression. She broke in to ask questions and to tell her own stories.

Happiness filled her, light and freeing. Aurelia recognized the feeling but from so long ago she could not believe it was real. Any moment it might flutter off with a meadowlark and leave her to cloudy seriousness.

The conversation went on and on, and the happiness floated inside her, remaining as she noted the passing of the day and the need to begin on the return journey. She got up to saddle Bianca, still listening as Robert described how his stallion had dropped a cocky hired hand on the paddock ground. "Sounds like Horizon is a good judge of character"—she laughed, then rethought her stance—"or maybe he's just loyal."

She tightened the girth and turned to hear her friend's response. But to her surprise, Robert had stood up just behind her. His eyes searched her face from less than a foot away. The proximity startled her, as did his intent expression. "Wait," he said. He reached out as if to take her hand, then pulled back, brushing her wrist with the backs of his trailing fingers.

Despite herself, her heart began pounding in her ears for the second time that afternoon. Her thoughts returned to the earlier moment by the creek bed, and her body longed to flee. But something even stronger demanded she stay.

"I know it's getting late, but there's something I need to say," he continued. "I can't afford to put it off any longer, as much as I'd like." His next words cut the haze. "I have a plan to capture the assassin and whoever is behind the plot."

Happiness drained in rapid descent.

"I've tried and tried to avoid this"—he kept talking—"but without a motive, I can't accuse either the king of Anthone or the queen of Tyralt. Every way I look at it, I get the same answer. I need you as bait."

Chapter Eleven
THE BAIT

A‌URELIA TRIED TO KEEP HER HANDS FROM TREM-bling as she entered her stepmother's dressing room. The day had dawned as beautifully as the day before, but the task ahead seemed to screen out the sunlight even better than the room's filmy curtains. Elise's frown shone in the vanity glass. Surely there was no real danger. Even if Elise was behind the plot, she would not dirty her own white hands with her stepdaughter's blood.

Nonetheless, the sight of Melony sent a wave of relief flowing through Aurelia's veins. *A brief reprieve.* The younger princess sat in a wicker chair beside the vanity table with her hands folded in her lap and her ankles neatly crossed. Her cheeks glowed like polished apples, and her green dress shimmered like garden leaves. She reminded Aurelia of an illustration in a children's book.

But Melony must not stay. A private talk was the only way to persuade Elise to let her guard down. Aurelia gathered her courage. "Excuse me, Mel, would you mind if I have a moment alone with your mother?"

"Of course not." Melony stood up, then moved close, clasping her sister's hands. *Are you all right?* she mouthed silently.

Aurelia nodded, trying to mask her fear, but she felt grateful when her sister's sharp tug pulled her into the hallway out of Elise's hearing. The queen's wintry face continued to frown at them from a portrait on the wall. "How did you dare?" Melony whispered, a tone of admiration in her voice.

"Dare?"

"I mean he's very handsome, but Father must be furious."

The scene in the throne room. Under the strain of acting out Robert's plan, Aurelia had forgotten about the public request for the picnic outing. It must be the talk of the palace by now. "Father gave his permission," she said.

Melony gave her a knowing look. "Yes, but he expected you to refuse."

"He just lectured me on how I should encourage my suitors. Besides, Robert is Henry's nephew."

"That's even worse." Melony sighed, leaning against the wall. "Now Father has to be careful not to upset Henry."

For some reason, the comment grated on Aurelia's nerves.

She disliked the implication that Robert was somehow less worthy than the myriad of suitors her sister allowed to call. "Look, I don't know why you're surprised. You receive notes from almost every young man in the palace."

Melony tilted her head. "But I don't accept them in public." Her voice scaled up. "The Vantauges aren't royal. They aren't even titled. Father would never accept a relationship between one of his daughters and . . . " The diatribe trailed off, replaced by an uneasy silence.

Aurelia stared at her sister, unsure what lay behind this unusual speech. "Mel, is something wrong?"

Her sister's fist rebounded off the wall a couple of times, and Melony gave a faint smile. "No. I . . . I guess I'm just realizing how limited our choices are as we grow older."

"Why? What's happened?" Aurelia tucked a loose gold curl behind her sister's ear.

"Oh, Father claims the populace is upset about the funds used for my coming-out party."

Was that all? Aurelia grinned. It was nice to know her frivolous sister was developing a civic conscience. "Never mind, Mel. Everyone deserves a birthday. Next year, maybe you can limit the guest list to no more than half the kingdom."

"Maybe." Melony lifted a hand. "But I wouldn't want to start a civil war." The blue eyes sparkled, and she turned to retreat down the hallway.

Aurelia wished her own problems were limited to party

expenses. She steeled herself for the coming encounter and returned to her stepmother's dressing room.

The queen remained at her vanity table, scrutinizing the rows of pearls in her hair. A silk robe draped over her nightdress, and satin slippers protected her feet. "My goodness," Elise said, her eyes tracing their way from her stepdaughter's bound hair to the pair of leather shoes on Aurelia's feet, "you girls are putting me to shame this morning. Of course I might be further along in my toilette without all these interruptions."

Aurelia bit her tongue, telling herself not to allow Elise's criticism to spoil the plan. "Your Majesty, someone mentioned you might have heard of a Geordian Desert racehorse in Tyralt City."

Elise's hand jolted, causing an ivory hairbrush to skid across the table. Her smooth face reflected nothing. "Really, my dear, that sounds like court gossip. What did this source say the horse looked like?"

"Golden, he said. He seemed certain about the color."

"And well he might, as that seems to be the only correct part of his story. I believe a golden racehorse has entered the area. One of your father's colleagues told me of it. Perhaps he shared his information with your young man." Elise planted the word *young* in the conversation.

Aurelia ignored it. "I should like to see the colt race."

"I heard it would not be racing here."

"So he said." Aurelia pouted, plopping into the wicker chair and knocking several pillows onto the floor. She looked up, widening her eyes in a pleading expression. "I wondered if you could use your influence to persuade the owner to change his or her mind."

Elise frowned at the displaced pillows. "I am certain I could do so, but I am not certain holding a horse race would be a good use of that influence. Perhaps the owner does not wish to put the horse on display."

"True. That is why I thought you could invite the colt and its rider to come to the palace arena for a private run." The word *private* dropped from Aurelia's lips with emphasis.

"I suppose that might be managed." Elise dipped her fingers into a jar of lotion and smoothed the pale substance into her hands. "With a limited audience, the owner's worries might be resolved."

"No one from the palace would be there except a jockey and me."

"Are you certain you can promise that, Aurelia? I won't have the owner upset because of your little scheme."

"Promise."

Elise gave a dramatic sigh. "The horse belongs to the king of Anthone. You may take your proposal to him." She turned back to her mirror. "Now, I really must prepare for breakfast, my dear. You have made me dreadfully late."

Aurelia stood up, retrieved the fallen pillows, and put them in their proper places. "Sorry I kept you." She struggled to maintain a slow pace as she moved toward the door.

"Don't be surprised if he refuses." The queen's brittle voice followed her out.

Free of her stepmother's gaze, Aurelia hurried down the hall, her mind spinning. Elise had approved of the private race, but then she had named Edward of Anthone. What did that mean? Was the queen behind the plot, or was Edward? Were they behind it together? Without answers, there was only one course of action.

Pausing just long enough to collect Minuet as a chaperone, Aurelia headed down the corridor of the west wing. Edward had been placed at the far end of the hall, as far away from the royal family's rooms in the east wing as possible.

She rapped on the door.

"Enter," said a deep voice.

"Your Majesty?" She eased into the dark sitting room. Not a single window split the green brocade on the walls. The oak desk in the corner and the bookshelf beside the doorway did nothing to brighten the room, and the four chairs at the center were murky brown. "May I speak with you?" Aurelia asked.

Keen eyes watched her entrance. "Certainly, Your Highness." Edward ducked his bald head in slow acknowledgment. "What a pleasant surprise." His tongue slid suggestively over the word *pleasant.*

She struggled not to cringe. "I've heard talk about a golden colt that has entered the area. My stepmother tells me he belongs to you."

The pink skin on Edward's forehead pressed together in thin wrinkles. "Indeed," he said, gesturing to the high-backed chair at his side. "I was not aware the colt's presence had become common knowledge."

She sat tentatively on the chair's slick cushion. "Keeping a good racehorse a secret is a task too great for even a man of your wealth and reputation."

His chin dipped forward, jogging the layers of loose skin along his neck. "I had heard Your Highness values good horses."

"I am only interested in the best."

"I assure you I collect the very best for my stable." He stood up, keeping her under his predatory gaze.

Her flesh crawled. "That's easy to say with the colt hidden away. Are you willing to prove it?"

He glided around her, circling with unexpected ease for a man of his age. "Are you challenging me, Your Highness?"

"Making an invitation, rather." She lifted her chin. "I would like to see your colt race. I understand you do not want him to perform in public, but I thought you might allow him a private run in the royal arena."

A thin smile cracked his face. "A private run against another horse?"

"One," she replied. "A single stallion, a jockey, and myself as the audience."

He stopped circling and stepped closer. His rancid breath blew on her forehead. "Your father and I have yet to complete our business. I have no time for watching horse races."

One less complication. "Your Majesty's presence will be missed, but if the colt has as much potential as you claim, he may manage to run without it."

Edward reached out and ran his index finger in a slow curve along her jaw. "I will consider your request and send you a written note if it can be arranged."

She shivered. And fled.

Not half an hour later, Robert hurried toward the guest rooms himself, pushing his cousin in front of him. Chris jerked away. "Robert, this is insane. Why am I doing this?"

"Think of it as a favor," Robert hedged, pretending to look at the portraits between the doors lining the corridor. He needed someone's help, and he wasn't going to let Aurelia walk into Edward's rooms after hearing about her last visit. The man was too unpredictable.

Chris banged his right fist with the flat of his left palm. The sound echoed down the empty hallway. "I am reminded of the time when we were children and we built the fort."

"With the chairs?"

"And Uncle Brian's table with the family crest." Chris gave his cousin a look.

"Hmm." Robert lowered his eyes, trying to avoid the critical gaze. Floral patterns flashed beneath his feet.

"I was in charge of defending the fort," Chris said, slowing his walk, "and you were the invading force."

"As I recall, you appointed me to invade the fort."

"You invaded, all right. You busted your father's table into three pieces."

"Poor structural quality," Robert defended himself. He hated to think what might happen if his current plan failed. The results would be far more tragic than a broken table. He tugged his cousin forward.

"And I took the blame because you were afraid your father would be disappointed in you."

"I remember."

"Well, believe me." Chris closed a firm hand on Robert's shoulder. "Your father's reaction was nothing next to my father's when he saw that dent in the coat of arms yesterday."

Robert looked up, feeling guilty. He had forgotten all about that. Between the picnic outing and his plans to trap the assassin, not to mention Uncle Henry's busy schedule, Robert had not even crossed his uncle's path. "Did you tell him I caused it?"

"He didn't exactly wait for me to explain. I think you're the one who owes *me* the favor."

"Then don't think of this as a favor," said Robert, opening a palm and closing it in a fist. "Think of it as an opportunity."

"For what, getting caught where I don't belong?" Despite the protest, Chris's face glowed with anticipation.

"Aren't you the one who said getting into trouble allows you to get your father's attention?" Robert teased.

"Yes, but I had enough of it yesterday." They stopped outside the door to King Edward's rooms, and Chris dropped his voice. "What am I supposed to do?"

"Just go in and distract Edward. Once I'm hidden inside, make sure he leaves the room. I don't know how much time I'll need. Maybe ten minutes."

"What if there is someone else in the room?"

"There won't be."

Chris tapped a hand on the brass door latch. "How do you know that?"

Because no one else was in the room thirty minutes ago when Aurelia came out. "Then take whoever else is in the room out with you as well."

"How am I supposed to do that?"

Robert shrugged in exasperation and slid against the wall to avoid being seen. "You have more experience with this sort of thing than I do."

"Right." Sarcasm filled the syllable. Then, without giving warning, Chris barged into the sitting room. "Your Majesty."

"Yes?" Edward's voice vibrated with tension. Robert could

see the man's angry face through the crack in the doorway. "And you are?"

"Your afternoon guide." Chris slid forward, drawing the king's eyes toward the far side of the room.

"I don't need a guide. I've visited here since before you were born." Edward turned his back to the door.

And Robert moved, slipping through the doorway and squeezing his body behind an upright bookcase. Aurelia had been right about that, *the perfect hiding place.* A small gap beside a bookend provided an excellent viewing spot.

Once secure, Robert returned his attention to the conversation in the room. Chris had leaped into the challenge as expected. "The king said I must show you the new guest wing. He's certain you'll want to stay there as soon as it's complete."

What new guest wing?

"I can wait until it's finished to see it," said Edward.

"Oh no, His Majesty wants your advice. After all, what more important guest could he have than the leader of the neighboring kingdom?" Chris's wagging tongue coaxed Edward out of the room. The door swung shut behind them.

Robert launched into motion, out from behind the oak bookshelf, to the desk in the corner. Not a single item lingered on the stained surface. His hand flew to a drawer handle and froze.

"Odd how the king did not mention that." Edward's voice echoed through the wall.

No, no, not yet.

The voice drifted away. "Yes, I have all sorts of ideas."

Robert's fingers flew back into action. One drawer after another opened at his touch: ink, parchment, quill pens. *There it was!* Exactly the item he had been looking for, right in the center of the top drawer.

He snatched it, folded it, and hid it in the pocket beneath his coat.

Aurelia shivered and adjusted the loose sides of her cloak, pulling them tight. A chill wind gusted over the private balcony, taking with it the last of the warm weather; and a dark cloud drifted in from the east, stretching out its talons and burying the sinking sun. She could not help but feel that the weather had adapted to her emotions.

She wished she were back on the sunny meadow, racing horses or telling stories. Or feeling her heart ricochet at Robert's kiss. Anything but standing here discussing his plan for capturing the culprit behind the plot. "But if Horizon has never run on a course, are you certain you want to race him against the golden colt?" she asked.

"I have no intention of racing him," Robert said, leaning on the balcony railing. "And yes, I want him at the racecourse in case I have to chase down Gregory."

"How do you know Gregory will be the colt's rider?"

"He's a jockey. I can tell by the way he's built. And he was the one riding the colt the night I went to Midbury. Both our suspects are connected with him. Whether Edward or Elise is behind the plot, Gregory tried to kill you on Carnival night. The culprit would be a fool to involve someone else when he or she could hire the same assassin."

"What if neither Edward nor Elise takes the bait?" Aurelia asked, glancing back through the balcony curtains toward her sitting room. In order to gain the chance to talk in private, she had sent her lady's maid on a pointless errand. The room remained empty.

"Then I shall have to come up with another plan," Robert said. "But I think the culprit will be unable to resist the chance..."

"To kill me when I'm trapped alone in that arena." Aurelia's eyes turned back to the view beyond the balcony's edge. Stable walls stretched below her, and behind them stood the massive stone wall encompassing the racecourse. Even from this height, she could not see into the arena's center.

"You will not be alone," Robert said. "I will be there, and your father will be hidden behind the curtains of the royal box. I need you to saddle Horizon and bring him to the arena for me. I won't have time while I'm hiding the king. Unless you prefer to be the one to tell your father about the plan?"

She shuddered and shook her head. In her mind, she could see her father's reaction when he learned about the danger in which she was placing herself. "Why do we have to involve my father at all?"

"Because he should hear the instigator's name from the assassin's own lips."

Wind tugged at her cloak, and she pushed it down over her skirts. "If we can hide my father, why can't we hide one or two guards as well?"

"Because we want Gregory to feel safe, like he is the one in control. If he thinks we're the only ones who know he's the assassin, he might tell us who hired him. He'll think he still has a chance to escape." Robert looked her in the eye. "He won't feel that way with a couple of guards holding him at sword point. Do you really think palace guards are going to stay hidden once they know an assassin is near the crown princess?"

Memories of the incident in the market square flashed into Aurelia's mind. "No, I suppose not." She could not keep a waver of anxiety from creeping into her voice.

The brush of Robert's fingers touched her cheek. "I'll be there before you arrive." His voice scratched as though holding back emotion. "I promise." He held her gaze, and the moment stretched.

And stretched. She might as well have been standing on the balcony railing. What precipice could hold more danger than his gaze? Or incite a more powerful urge to jump?

"E-excuse me, Your Highness," squeaked a voice. Minuet stood behind them, holding a white envelope in her trembling hand. "I am to deliver this."

Aurelia blushed, afraid her thoughts had been printed on her face. She took the sealed parchment and flipped it over. *No label.* Her fingers shook as she managed to break the wax. A single written line met her gaze.

Tomorrow morning at seven o'clock in the arena

Someone had taken the bait. A sour taste lodged in her throat as the paper slipped from her fingers.

Robert snatched it before it blew away. His eyes devoured the words and lifted to the lady's maid. "Is the messenger who delivered this still here?"

Minuet shook her head.

"Do you know the messenger?" he demanded. "Does he or she work for the queen? Or Edward of Anthone?"

The girl backed away, no doubt shaken by the sudden onslaught of questions. "I . . . I did not recognize the messenger."

"Was it a man or a woman?"

Minuet's face paled.

"What did the messenger look like?"

"Enough." Aurelia put a hand out to stop Robert. "Never mind him," she told the lady's maid. "You may return to your duties. Lay out a gown for tomorrow."

The girl scurried away.

Robert thrust the message at Aurelia. "If the handwriting matches either Elise's or Edward's, we have written evidence. Do you recognize the writing? Does it belong to your stepmother?"

The message's neat print put Elise's scrawl to shame. Aurelia shook her head. "It must be from King Edward."

Robert pulled a paper from his pocket. Aurelia craned her neck to see the writing sample he had stolen from Edward's desk. The lettering on the paper ran together in an even sloppier fashion than the queen's.

Neither one.

Chapter Twelve

THE RACE

THE MINUTE HAND ON THE TALL CASE CLOCK IN THE waiting room clicked forward, 6:40 A.M. Tension crept up Robert's spine, and nerves floated in his hollow stomach. The king's schedule should have remained empty until nine o'clock, but muffled voices hummed behind the official chamber door. Someone had disrupted the king's morning even before Robert's arrival at 6 A.M. And judging by the rising and falling of the voices, the discussion was not going well.

Again the minute hand clicked. Robert gathered his courage. He was going to have to interrupt the meeting. Aurelia was saddling his horse in the stables at this very minute, and he had promised her he would be at the arena before she arrived. He raised a hand to knock on the door.

Another hand clapped onto his raised elbow, halting the

knock in midair. "There you are," said Chris. "I've been looking all over for you." Robert blinked. He had been so anxious about the task before him, he had not even seen his cousin enter the room. "I finally wake up in time to practice with you, and you aren't on the field."

Unbuckling the sword belt at his hip, Chris dropped into a cushioned chair. Clearly he had every intention of staying. "I sure hope you found what you needed yesterday," he continued. "I don't think King Edward will ever follow me again. You should have seen his face when I showed him that old rubble pile by the sheep barns and told him it was the site of the new guest wing. He looked prepared to vomit." Chris leaned back in his chair and propped his feet on a footstool. "Maybe that will keep him from returning here in the future."

Robert glanced back and forth between the clock and the closed chamber door. Of all the times for his cousin to wake up at the crack of dawn. "Listen, Chris, I'm sorry, but I have to meet Aurelia in a few minutes. She and I have an appoint—"

"No, you don't, not until eight o'clock. She wanted me to tell you someone was detained and wouldn't be able to make it to the racecourse until then. I'd never have found you if she hadn't sent me here to deliver the message."

Robert let out a breath. Another hour. Perhaps he could catch the king without interrupting the argument behind the closed door. But he needed to rid himself of his cousin first.

Chris's silver sword hilt gleamed on the floor. *The perfect excuse.* "Listen," Robert said, "I only have my real sword with me, but if you run upstairs and grab me a practice weapon, I might have a few minutes to spare."

Chris laughed. "Between appointments with His Majesty and Her Royal Highness? I doubt it."

"Still worried I might damage your perfect reputation?"

Nothing worked like a challenge to the ego. "All right." Chris headed toward the open doorway, then stopped. "Almost forgot, Father wanted me to give you this. It came for you this morning." He handed Robert a sealed envelope and departed.

Robert stared at the paper in his hand. His own name stared back in his father's bold script. Unsteady fingers broke the seal, and the parchment opened in three pages.

Dear Robert,

Though I did not want you to return to the palace, I regret allowing you to do so without my support. I hope you are successful and that you know my anger stemmed from a father's desire to protect his son.

I failed to prepare you at the time of your departure for the task ahead; therefore, I have enclosed a number of details in this letter which may help you solve your case. As a spy for the king, I gained knowledge about the royal family which is not well-known. Please use discretion in how you share the information.

The letter went on with line after line of details Robert had never been told. Halfway through the third paragraph, he stopped. His eyes read and reread the same sentence, the words blaring off the page. There it was. The motive.

He looked up toward the window, his thoughts swirling with the news and its implications for the young woman preparing to meet him at the palace arena. A veil of fog and early-morning mist obscured his view.

The cold mist soaked into the stockings above Aurelia's boots and drizzled under the neck of her riding jacket. Her eyes glanced up to the stallion she led at her side, then traced the inner edge of the ominous arena wall surrounding her. *Where is he?* She tried to force herself to relax her death grip on Horizon's reins, but her fingers disobeyed.

Maybe something had happened to Robert. *He wouldn't let anything happen. He wouldn't leave me alone with this man. He wouldn't.*

But he had.

A golden two-year-old colt cantered along the course's surface. The morning drizzle had softened the earth, and dark clods flew up as hooves dug a fresh pathway. Perched on the colt's back sat a man matching Robert's description of Marcus Gregory.

Aurelia's eyes followed him, noting his long dark coat and the way he sat straight up in the saddle. The colt turned in her direction, and she squelched the urge to flee back to the stables. Gregory must have spotted her.

She could not panic and ruin the plan. *Robert will be here,* she told herself, sweeping one last look around the arena. Wooden seats climbed up into the fog along the rim of the gray wall, and a wide, grassy field, once used for jousting matches, stretched across the vacant center. A dirt racecourse surrounded the field in an oblong loop. And wooden barriers separated the course from both the seating area and the field. Resounding emptiness.

Except for the approaching colt with the assassin on its back. Aurelia moved up against the belly of the stallion beside her. She had not anticipated riding Horizon at all, but with Gregory nearly on top of her, the stallion's back beckoned like high ground. She mounted.

Gregory's beady eyes and long nose overpowered his other features as he rode up to her. He inclined his head. "It is a pleasure to accept your invitation to ride this morning, Your Highness."

For the first time in her life, Aurelia was thankful subjects bowed rather than shook hands. She pulled Horizon a pace backward. There was no room for a sword under those riding clothes, but Gregory might have a dagger, a silent weapon that would allow him to escape before someone discovered the deed.

She must stall for time. "Your mount is truly stunning. Do tell me, what is his background?"

Gregory slid a hand over his dull blond hair. "I'm afraid I have only had the honor of riding him recently, Your Highness."

A feeble attempt to hedge around the question, she thought. "And who is your employer?"

"I have had more than one employer this year." He tilted his head. "But I am now under contract with a young woman of some standing." *A lie.* Unless one thought of Elise as young. Gregory himself could not yet have reached his late twenties.

"And what is your name, sir?"

"Marc Gregory." The truth seared worse than the lie.

Enough. She had invited him in the guise of wanting to see the colt race. As there was no other rider present, she must pretend to be doing the racing—at least until Robert arrived. "I require a few minutes to prepare my mount," she said. "He must warm his muscles before I can run him."

"Yes, Your Highness." Gregory's feral breath made her choke as the man neared her side. Again she pulled away. He had too easily accepted the concept of her riding. Despite her expertise, most riders had to be persuaded to race against a woman, and she had told Anthone she would be the audience. Had Gregory known she would be alone? Had someone stopped Robert from joining her? Had someone harmed him?

A chill glided through her chest as she guided Horizon away from the arena's entryway. A desire to flee back through the opening tugged at her. But the gate was shut. She would have to dismount to open it. And she could not do so with any sense of security. She had closed the thick carved sides to give Gregory the illusion of control. The trap tightened around her.

Her frantic mind sought another escape route. At the far end of the arena, the royal box jutted out to the very edge of the course. Dark blue curtains hung without movement, pulled shut. The earlier dread of her father's presence behind those curtains paled beneath the blunt knowledge that no one was there. Regardless, the exit inside the private box would be even more difficult to access than the main gate. A high barrier separated her from the inside.

She walked Horizon around on the dirt surface of the course as long as she could, clinging to every second. Still Robert did not come. The lines of Gregory's face hardened until postponing the race no longer seemed wise.

"A loop and a half?" he asked, and she nodded. The last half did not matter. She needed a lead before the end of the first loop, a lead big enough to give her time to dismount and open the gate. She must get out ahead and break away.

Her mind spun in haunting repetition as she drew up beside the post at the start. *He is going to kill me. He is going to kill me. He is going to kill me.*

Wrinkles of concentration popped out on Gregory's forehead as he grasped the reins and waited for the sign to go. A golden head tossed at the grip. Horizon also tugged for release. She pried her hand off Horizon's neck and lifted her arm to signal the start. Then let it fall.

Hooves, and muscles, and pounding earth. Horizon took his head immediately, and she let him have it. Tension ripped from her chest in the form of an uncontrollable scream urging him to go as she had never begged any horse. She did not know where she would go if she escaped the imprisoning wall. The future mattered only if she pulled ahead.

Horizon had never run a real race, never even run on a course, according to Robert. The stallion ran now, not as a racehorse setting his pace, but as she needed him to run, as a competitor trying to break the spirit of the younger animal at his side.

The colt's spirit did not break. It held its own, flying out at the same unrestrained speed. It also was no typical racehorse. It also laid claim to desert bloodlines; and if its stamina held as Horizon's did, she could not pull ahead, perhaps not even enough to win the race, much less get a lead.

Neck and neck. Gregory had not shifted from his rider's stance. If his horse was like Horizon, he expected his mount's stamina to hold out and give him the lead later in the race. They ran the whole first turn head-to-head, shoulder to shoulder, flank to flank.

Cold morning air numbed Aurelia's face, contrasting with the terrible heat burning her chest. She ducked down and swore to herself to ride smart. Forcing her eyes off her competitor, she urged Horizon on. At the sight of the return stretch, the stallion launched forward and began to pull away. Aurelia closed her eyes and breathed, willing herself to feel an increase in velocity.

When she opened her eyes, she glanced under her arm to see if Horizon had managed to form a lead. And her heart slammed up to her throat.

Sure enough, the golden colt now lagged a foot and a half behind, but with that change the calm demeanor on Gregory's face had disappeared. He had lifted out of his normal riding stance and was leaning forward. Aurelia barely had time to note his approach before a hand reached out to grab at her. In horror she realized how he intended to kill her.

It was to be an accident. Here on the racecourse. She would be trampled, or perhaps her neck would break, and who could ever prove her death was anything but a tragic error in judgment on her own part? Of course he would trample her. Had he not attempted to do so only a week before?

His rough hand grasped at her shoulder, and slipped off. She must not allow him to force her from her mount. The ground blurred beneath Horizon's hooves, a fast pathway to death. Anger bloomed full on Gregory's face.

Horizon continued forward at full speed. Again Gregory leaned forward, this time even farther as his horse lost ground. The assassin clutched at her rib cage. She twisted sharply, maintaining her tight hold on the stallion. Again Gregory's hand slipped. He stood up in the stirrups and lunged to pull her off with his own weight.

But Horizon had had enough. Without her guidance, the stallion veered away from the treacherous rider. A tight clasp gripped Aurelia's ankle. Fear replaced thought. Gregory's grip held firm even as the assassin came unseated. Terrible seconds.

Then he fell, colliding with her mount, and Horizon stumbled. Still, his grip held, a deadly weight sucking her toward darkness.

And the weight dropped away. She heard a horrible crack as hooves scrambled over the body. Horizon swerved to the outside and regained his footing. Instead of continuing down the course, he rose up on his hind limbs and screamed.

Terrified of what she might find but afraid to keep her eyes off her attacker, Aurelia turned back toward the fallen man. The golden colt had continued to run. Gregory lay on the ground alone, not ten feet away. Injured, but not dead. Though he lay flat, the assassin reached into his coat with his right hand. Fresh fear glided through Aurelia's veins. Her eyes focused on the hand: the hand pulling an object from the coat, the hand gripping the hilt of a pistol, the hand aiming the muzzle.

In that instant, Aurelia changed. This man intended to kill her. She had known this for what felt like a lifetime, and she had tried to reason herself a way out. Reason shattered. She crouched low on Horizon's neck and urged the stallion forward.

Horizon leaped like a gush of blood from a main artery. Gregory moved too slowly to get off a single shot as raging hooves lifted and slammed upon him—once, twice, three times, four. Aurelia held on, blocking out the screams from man and horse until Horizon drew back, pacing away. Only then, as she let her eyes drop to the broken, bleeding body, did her hands relinquish their death grip on the stallion's reins. Her body slipped to the ground. Her feet could not hold her. And she collapsed on the course.

Chapter Thirteen
THE DUEL

THE DISCUSSION BEHIND THE CHAMBER DOOR ceased. Robert turned to see who had usurped so much time, and warning tingled up his arms as Edward of Anthone swept out into the waiting room. Sharp eyes met Robert's, a thin line of recognition creasing Edward's lips. Without a word, the Anthonian king brushed by in departure.

Robert watched, baffled. Strange that Edward would notice him, much less recognize him.

"Robert Vantauge?" Aurelia's father stood in the chamber doorway. Dark crescents lined the bottoms of his eyes, and tension filled his face. "Waiting to ask permission for another pleasure jaunt?" His weak smile did little to lighten the tone.

"Your Majesty, I can explain."

"I should hope so. Actions in court rarely end on the day they are presented, young man. The repercussions can cause great damage."

"But I don't have time now." Robert braced himself for the king's reaction. "I need you to come with me, Your Majesty, to the royal arena. The sooner we depart, the better. I promised Aurelia I would be there before the assassin arrives."

"Aurelia knows about the assassin?" a familiar voice echoed from outside the hallway, and Chris entered, sans the extra practice sword.

Thanks, cousin, your timing is uncanny today.

Robert sighed as the blood of anger rushed into the king's face, and gray eyebrows spiked in slicing accusation. "You would place my daughter in harm's way?"

"Your Majesty," said Robert, "your daughter is in harm's way every moment of every day until the instigator is caught." He met the king's gaze. "She understands that. Do you?"

Chris shifted uncomfortably. "You've set a trap?"

"I believe the assassin will arrive at the arena within the half hour," Robert answered. "Prior to his arrival, I would like Your Majesty hidden behind the curtains of the royal box."

Silence replaced accusation. The clicking of the clock filled the void, and Robert could feel time slipping away. Perhaps Aurelia had been correct. Perhaps he should never have come here. But how could he convince this man to arrest the culprit without evidence? And there was no evidence stronger than the power of one's own sight. "Your Majesty, please come with me."

Measuring eyes traveled up and down Robert's body. "I want guards stationed around the arena to ensure her safety," said the king.

"There is no time or way to hide men in those seats," Robert replied. "Please come now."

Hesitation, then a brief nod. "Lead the way."

Robert adjusted his sword belt on his way out of the waiting room. The light casing hugged his waist, and the pommel felt smooth under the tight clench of his right hand. His cousin's quick footsteps attached themselves to Robert's heels. "Chris, you can't come. I'll see you this afternoon."

"You have lost your mind if you think I'm going to let you walk into this snake pit without me. If there's room behind those box curtains for His Majesty, there's room for me." Chris placed a palm on the hilt of his sword. "Besides, I was always better with one of these than you."

No point in arguing. They hurried down the stairs and out around the stables toward the arena. The early-morning fog had risen, taking with it the drizzling mist, but clouds hovered in a thick mass, holding down the morning chill. Boots left footprints in the damp soil.

The gate was shut. Odd. It had been open when Robert had inspected the site. For now he skirted the main entryway, heading instead to the private entrance on the opposite end of the arena.

A locked padlock sealed the door. The king reached below

his collar and pulled out a large metal key on a chain. *The key of Tyralt,* Robert thought, *the only master key on the palace grounds.* Passed from leader to leader on the deathbed of the reigning monarch, it was a symbol of succession as well as of Tyralian security. *Click.*

The king led the way into a narrow tunnel under rows of raised seats. Light filtered through cracks, and water dripped halfheartedly from support beams. Wooden stairs creaked as three pairs of shoes climbed the boards. Stepping into the private box, Robert reached for the curtains.

A scream shattered the calm as the fabric separated. Halfway across the arena, two horses flew side by side, less than a length apart. The golden colt chased Horizon, the stallion's scream still reverberating off the stone wall. Robert didn't have to see the riders' faces to know who they belonged to: Marcus Gregory and Aurelia.

Already here. Horror slid in sheets up Robert's insides, clamping down on his throat. He was late, and there was no time for thought or reason or anything else because Gregory had leaped forward and was trying to bring Aurelia down, down under the swirling hooves.

Robert forgot about his plan, about the king beside him and the cousin behind him. Using a hand for leverage, he leaped over the high barrier separating the box from the racecourse. Down, down he dropped, a six-foot fall. His bent knees absorbed the impact, and he held his footing.

Raising his head, he found Horizon. No time. He just ran, with all the speed he could manage toward his horse, toward Aurelia.

But the course was designed for racehorses, not human beings. The distance stretched in threatening agony. He hurtled over the short barrier that divided the dirt ring from the inner field and began the marathon across the grass. His legs pumped over the level surface, unable to appreciate the smoothness. The distance taunted him like a mountain with a false top. *And what can you do when you get there? An exhausted man on foot?*

He glanced up, and shock seared his spine. Horizon had turned around. The horse stood with front hooves upraised, still screaming. Then came down, heavily. Desperate to see, Robert ran on, closer and closer. The stallion reared again and came back down, pounding and pounding the object below.

A shattered body in the dirt. Then another body, slipping off Horizon's back and tumbling to the ground. *Aurelia.*

Robert came over the barrier, crashing on his knees beside her. Her brown hair splayed down; her body bent forward, chest over her knees, hands on her head. Her torso heaved. Air rushed in gasps, of fear, or relief. *Alive.*

He grabbed her shoulders and pulled her to him. Wrapping his arms around her back, he crushed her head to his chest. They didn't speak.

For minutes. Then her dark eyes lifted, gazing at him through strands of tangled hair. "Where were you?" she managed, her voice trembling with emotion.

His eyes closed in the face of that look. "I received your message to wait until eight o'clock. I didn't think you would be here yet."

She pulled back, holding his upper arms for support, then cut him like a dagger with her words. "What message?"

Realization dawned through a haze. She had sent no message. There had been no delay. Gregory had arrived at seven o'clock. The message had been a sham, designed to do exactly what it had done, keep Robert from the arena.

He untangled himself from Aurelia's arms, pulling back and rising to his feet. There must be many ways the deception could have been achieved, but only one presented itself now. *Chris lied.*

As the thought blazed into consciousness, Robert staggered, caught his balance, and turned to look at the men he had left behind. The king had made his way to the bottom of the public seats and collapsed. At his side stood Chris, a long arm wrapped around the older man's shoulders as if in comfort.

Comments and events flooded back into Robert's mind: Aurelia's statement during the picnic that she and Chris had never been close, Chris's failure to deliver the message Robert had tried to send, Chris's failure to ever bring back information on Marcus Gregory or Edward of Anthone. Chris had been with Aurelia the night of Carnival. He had disappeared before the attack. He had seen her disguise.

No! Robert wanted to lay a gray veil over it all. Bury the memories below the surface, where they could once again be treated as harmless anecdotes, the actions of his well-meaning, irresponsible cousin. His *cousin*. Didn't that stand for something?

Robert looked at the young woman crumpled on the ground beside him, then at the lifeless flesh and bone trampled into the dirt. Not in the face of this, he realized. There was no way to replace the veil after something like this.

He took a step forward, then turned back to Aurelia. She remained on the ground, her head once again buried under her arms, sobs now echoing from her body. She needed an explanation, he knew, but she had been through enough for now. And the danger was not yet past, not with a traitor standing across the stadium, an arm resting on her father's shoulder.

"Wait here for several minutes," Robert said. "Then stand and leave through the gate as fast as you can. Find guards and send them here. Do you understand?"

Tearstains lined the dirt on her cheeks as she looked up in bewilderment. How could she understand anything after the horror she had been through? He repeated the directions.

She nodded, looking as though she wanted to ask him something but had no words.

He could not answer her anyway. He needed to return to the king. Now. From this distance, the king and Chris couldn't see the bodies on the ground or tell that Aurelia still breathed. They would assume the crown princess was dead, especially if Robert returned at a slow walk.

He traversed the field, the same painful thought repeating with each step. *My cousin. My cousin. My cousin.* Another step. Another. He neared the two figures at the base of the seating area.

The king waited in serious distress. Collapsed upon the lowest row of seats, he stared into nothingness, a sickening gray shade tinting his face. His right hand shook disjointedly without purpose.

Chris vaulted over the barrier and came forward, wrapping an arm around his cousin's right shoulder in a brief clasp. Robert endured the embrace, then slid away, stepping toward the king as if to ease the older man's grief. Instead he positioned himself between the distraught man and Chris, then rotated rapidly on the ball of his foot.

"You need not grieve, Your Majesty." Robert faced his cousin but spoke to the king. "Your daughter is alive."

The sound of a loud sob broke, but Robert had no time to direct his attention toward the king. For a split second, Chris's eyes flitted to the side before reining themselves in. "Thank Tyralt! Robert, why didn't you tell us right away? And why didn't you return to us immediately? His Majesty and I feared the worst."

"There was no message."

Robert watched the words sink in, then continued: "An hour ago, you came to me with a message you claimed was from Aurelia, saying that Marcus Gregory had been delayed. If you had not shared this with me, the king and I would have been here in time to avoid Gregory's attack. But Gregory and Aurelia arrived at seven o'clock. And Aurelia never gave you a message."

"Rob, what are you saying?" said Chris. "I gave you the message as I was given it."

"The message you were given from someone other than Aurelia, someone who wanted you to make sure I wasn't here on time. Yes, I know because that is the only way you could have known about our meeting on the course today. I didn't tell you until after you gave me the message. Aurelia didn't tell you. Only the person planning to have Aurelia killed would have permitted her to set up a private race without any security. Aurelia planted the bait on purpose, you see."

"You know who hired the assassin?" Chris said, his voice strangled.

"Yes," Robert lied, "but I did not know until a few minutes ago that you were a traitor."

Chris drew his sword with the rapid reflex of an expert. The sharp tip of the blade gleamed in the light. This was no practice sword.

But neither was Robert's. It also swished from its scabbard with startling ease.

The gamble of the lie paid off. Chris spoke: "Melony said you would never suspect her."

Melony? The name sliced through the arena. Not the queen. Not Edward. *Melony*. Chris had not been spending all his time flirting with Melony's lady's maids and friends from court. He had been spending it with the princess herself. "Why?" Robert asked. "Why would you help her?"

"I would have thought you of all people would understand, Rob," Chris said. "You've fallen just as hard for her sister."

Beauty. Beauty had always been Chris's weakness, and the blond princess was as beautiful as temptation. And as persuasive. "What did she promise you, Chris? A perfumed rejection letter if you helped murder her sister?"

Chris's sword leaped to life, aiming for the heart. But Robert had planted the barb, and he was prepared. He turned sharply to avoid the path of the blade. His sword flung the other away.

With the change in position, he caught a glimpse of the king. The older man stood, the blank gaze and tremble gone. This was a man who could reason and understand what he heard.

Chris moved to a neutral position, then flashed out in a feint off to the right.

Robert needled for information. "The night of Carnival, you were the one who told Gregory how to find Aurelia?"

"Of course, but you were the one who obtained the invitation." A wicked smile flashed across Chris's face. "She would never have invited me without you."

"And the girl in the starling costume?" *Tedasa, a friend of Melony's.*

"She was my ticket out of an unfortunate carriage accident."

Again the swords came forward and clashed, then slid apart, scraping steel against steel. The sound echoed in Robert's skull.

How many times had he heard that sound while crossing prac-tice swords with Chris? And how many times had they prac-ticed together even before they had steel practice swords? Chris had always been the better swordsman, always quicker, always stronger.

The two broke away, circling to the right. As they rotated, Robert caught sight of a movement over Chris's right shoulder. *Aurelia.* Robert wondered whether she had understood his direc-tions through her shock and if she would follow them if she had.

But he did not have time to watch because Chris had lunged forward again. Parry. Riposte. Parry. Slice. Chris moved up fast, whipping his sword in an arc, then pressing against Robert's steel blade. They stood, locked in position for nearly ten seconds, muscles straining. Robert changed his stance and thrust his cousin away.

Chris backed off. "It wasn't my idea to send for Uncle Brian. It was my father's, and I had no way of knowing you would come instead. By the time you arrived, I'd already promised Melony I'd help."

Commit murder. "I hope she valued that promise." Robert played for time, searching the background and breathing a little easier to see that Aurelia was indeed headed for the gate.

"I never thought you'd find out much of anything."

"Not with your help, you mean."

Chris swept in for a series of quick jabs, all of which Robert swept away. *Waste of effort.*

Neither he nor his cousin had yet attacked in earnest. Stalling, stalling, stalling. Somewhere outside the arena were soldiers, soldiers trained to obey the crown princess if she could just get out. Again Robert sought her with his eyes, and, sure enough, she was nearing the gate.

Now the swords clashed again. Chris reached out to the left, to the right, slow at first, then picking up speed. *He's testing me. He knows I've only been defending myself, and he wants to make sure I don't have any surprises in store before he starts his real offensive.* They had not practiced together since the day after Robert's return to the palace. Chris had never woken early enough until this morning.

He had not planned to practice this morning either—the realization hit. "You were prepared to fight with me today," Robert blurted.

"I had no intention of a fight. I had hoped you wouldn't bring your sword to a horse race. My way would have been much quicker."

Robert reeled from the verbal blow, and the traitor chose that moment to begin a genuine attack. The sword flew forward in sharp slashes. Chris's style: quick slashes followed by a powerful blow and repeated without abatement until the opponent crumbled under the onslaught.

Robert dropped his defensive pose. He did not wish to die this day, even if it meant attacking his cousin. As a heavy blow landed, Robert twisted to the right and slid his own weapon under his opponent's arm. The sword slid along Chris's side, but Chris also managed to glide away unharmed. A glare came Robert's way, hot with anger.

Now the swords flew. Up and arcing, low and jabbing, slicing across and down and always joined by the agile movement of the body.

Chris connected first, scratching below Robert's collarbone out and across the right shoulder. A hair deeper and Robert's sword arm might have fallen useless. As it was, Robert ignored the blood and retaliated with a sharp slice, sending Chris retreating rapidly. Robert pressed forward, refusing to allow his cousin the luxury of space.

Both fighters were now breathing hard and sweating. *Hurry, Aurelia!* Robert screamed in his mind. *Send someone. Please hurry!*

But even as he screamed, Chris's sword jabbed downward, this time at an angle. Gripping the sword with both hands, Chris brought all the strength he could muster in one thrust, straight for Robert's chest.

Robert rolled, hurling himself to the ground for the first time in the conflict. He brought his own sword up underneath the downward movement of the other and plunged his blade deep into the soft, unprotected flesh just below his cousin's rib cage. The sword slid upward at a sharp angle, through the liver . . .

And the heart.

Chapter Fourteen
CONFRONTATION

IN THE KING'S WAITING ROOM AGAIN, ROBERT'S tightly wrapped shoulder throbbed and his hands felt numb. He flexed his fingers, watching dull, pink nails flash in and out above the clean, beige linen of his shirtsleeves. Hot water and soap could not wash away the blood on his hands.

Murderer. He had not planned; he had not schemed; he had not dreamed of killing anyone, but he had committed the act.

Images from that morning scalded his vision: beneath him on the ground, the friend with whom he had teased and joked, trained and fought, cried and celebrated; Chris's chest struggling to heave up and down above the metal shaft; red liquid pooling on the churned earth; the blur of running guards in the distance;

the guards' hands lifting the fragile shell of the man Robert had killed, his cousin.

"Come in," a deep voice echoed from within the king's official chamber.

Robert stepped into the square room. Another day his jaw might have dropped at the ancient banners hanging from the ceiling, the medieval spear beneath the glass case, the royal coat of arms displayed with prominence. Instead he felt only the tightness of the windowless walls around him, the harsh stare of the king's gaze from behind the long oak desk, and the shock at seeing Aurelia.

She sat in a chair between him and the king, her back facing Robert. An elegant auburn dress flowed down from her neck to her ankles, white feathers skirting the hem. A foreign image, irreconcilable with the one scrawled on his brain: her brown eyes accusing him of being late.

He avoided those eyes as she twisted around. *Why was she here?* He had thought her father would protect her from reliving the morning's trauma. Then again, the last place Robert wanted to be was alone—alone where the cloak of anger, guilt, and powerlessness could render him motionless. Perhaps the same fear had chased her here.

"Your Majesty, you wished to see me?" Robert bowed, falling back on his childhood training to get through the moment.

"Indeed." The king's voice pounded like a gavel. "I find myself reeling. A man I hired uncovers a plot within my family and yet does not deem to tell me the nature of his discoveries." Aurelia shifted as though to argue, but her father held up a hand. "I expect to hear everything before either of you leaves this room. Young man, you may begin. Be sure to include how my daughter, whom I asked not to be informed of this investigation, came to know more about it than I."

Robert felt the room closing in around him. He had been summoned to account for actions he could no longer justify.

"Frankly, Father," Aurelia broke in, "I think *you* should begin. After all, you were the first of us aware of the plot."

The king pressed together the tips of his fingers, forming an arrow. For a moment Robert felt at a loss, unsure whether to speak or wait for the older man to do so. Then the king ended the suspense, dropping his hands to the sharp edge of the desk. "The first attempt on your life came over two months ago," he said to his daughter, launching into a recitation of the first two assassination attempts.

Robert listened with new ears, wondering what details his cousin had left out. When the king reached the part about the injured groom, Robert dared to interrupt. "Who had access to the damaged saddle?" he asked.

"The grooms, the stable hands," said the king.

"It is a beautiful saddle. Melony gave it to me as a gift," Aurelia added, saying this last as if it were a cherished detail.

She doesn't know. Why had the king not told her? Of what use were secrets now?

Robert struggled with his thoughts, unsure how to break the news as he took over the recitation. He shared the information about Chris's role in the Carnival-night accident but left out Melony's involvement. "The day of the horse fair," he said to Aurelia. "You told me you saw Chris in your parlor. Who was with him?"

"Tedasa," she answered.

"And Melony?"

"Of course. Why else would they have been in our parlor?"

Pieces, pieces, all slipping into place, all missed before. The king remained unreadable, his face a still carving, his thumb spinning a gold band on his left ring finger.

Robert continued with his story. When he reached the part about his trip to Midbury, Aurelia turned to her father. "Why did Edward of Anthone bring an illegal horse into Tyralt?" she asked.

"And what does he want from Your Majesty?" added Robert, hoping to finally receive an answer to that nagging question.

The king gave his daughter a stern look. "We will discuss King Edward in private."

Frustrated, Robert went on. "After my trip to Midbury, I tried to contact Aurelia. I must have left five messages with her lady's maid."

"Minuet, my new lady's maid?" Aurelia asked. "The one who used to work for Melony?"

No doubt she still does. "Yes." Robert realized the messages had not been screened by the queen at all, but had been passed on from a loyal servant to her previous mistress.

He skimmed over the day of the picnic, which brought him to this morning and his father's letter. "That's when I found the motive," he said, "a reason strong enough for someone to kill the crown princess." He hated to hurt her with the truth, but she had suffered enough from this secret. "At the time, I thought the culprit behind the plot might be the queen." He faced the king. "Your Majesty, Aurelia should know. The secret almost cost her her life."

Silence inflated the room. The king stared at his daughter, his face rigid. She waited, her eyes watching her father with expectation. Robert could hear their breathing.

Finally, the king spoke. "Melony is your sister, Aurelia. She stands next to inherit the throne."

"But... she can't." Aurelia shook her head. "She's not—"

"She's your blood sister, your half sister." The king's words dropped like bullets. "She is my daughter by birth."

Aurelia's jaw flexed. Robert wished he could comfort her, but there was no place for him in this discussion. It was between her father and her. Cold facts peeled from her lips. "Melony is only two years younger than me. When she was born, Elise had a husband, and my mother..."

"Your mother still lived here," said the king, flattening a palm on the top of his desk. "After my second marriage, Elise and I agreed to keep Melony's true parentage a secret rather than to further tarnish your mother's reputation."

Your own reputation, you mean, Robert thought.

"But Melony knew you were her real father?" asked Aurelia.

The king raised his chin. "I drew up an official document, just in case you failed to marry. Melony had to sign it when she came of age. Elise and I told her a few months before her birthday."

"Before the first assassination attempt?"

"Yes."

The emotions in Aurelia's dark eyes swirled. "Melony wanted me killed in order to become queen? But how could she have had me poisoned?"

Only at that moment did Robert realize he knew the answer. "Your new lady's maid," he said. "She moves without making any noise. She surprised us on the balcony, remember? In his letter, Uncle Henry said that the person who left the poison goblet had access to your rooms at night. Melony must have ordered her to leave the goblet there."

"Melony sends her girls on missions." Aurelia spoke in a haunted manner, as though repeating someone else's words. "She sends them to the kitchens to share her daily preferences."

"Then Minuet could have put the poison in the cake as well," Robert said.

Horror dawned on Aurelia's face. "She knew about the race.

She came with me when I left the bait with Edward. I needed a chaperone."

"And she brought you the message with the time for the race. She couldn't answer my questions because she was the messenger." Robert reached into his pocket and pulled out the note from the previous day. He stepped close, bending down to spread the paper open before Aurelia on the desk. "Now do you recognize the handwriting?"

Her thumb slid along the neat, clear letters, her thumbnail blooming white from pressure. "Melony's," she whispered. "I didn't recognize it before because I expected to see Elise's."

"We both allowed our expectations to impair our judgment," Robert said, sliding the paper toward her father. The king did not touch it. His face wore a severe expression.

Robert realized he was still bending over the princess and quickly backed away.

"But how did Gregory get involved in the plot?" Aurelia asked. "He works for Elise."

"Not any longer," the king broke in. "When Melony turned fifteen, she inherited Midbury: the estate, the horses, and the servants' contracts. I did ask her if someone from the stables could greet Edward on Carnival night so that arrangements might be made for the later delivery of his colt. I did not specify a driver."

Then Melony chose Gregory. He must have delivered

Edward, then rendezvoused with her and Chris before orchestrating the carriage accident. Robert's head ached.

The pain further increased as Aurelia shared her own version of the morning, every word unfolding in a hollow tone. Robert winced as she explained why she had shut the gate.

If only he had not stressed the importance of the assassin feeling safe.

If only she had looked for Robert's presence before she shut that gate.

If only—

Too late now for ifs. They both had a death on their conscience. They would both face the same guilt in their sleep that night and in the nights to come.

But at least *they* would wake up. Robert gathered his strength, then told about his cousin's part in the plot as well as Chris's relationship with Melony. "Chris assumed I'd never find out Aurelia hadn't sent the message about the time delay. He thought she would be dead before I arrived at the racecourse."

"And if I wasn't," she whispered, "he planned to kill you."

"And me." The king stood up. "Which is why I am prepared to allow you to leave, Robert Vantauge, without having you arrested for placing my daughter in undue danger. You saved my life today, but your task is complete. You will return to your home. I do not want to see you on palace grounds again." The last words hung in the air, a judgment passed down from the leader of Tyralt.

Aurelia heard the door close following Robert's departure. *I should stop him,* she thought. *I should say something.* But her mind was frayed, tangled and torn, and on the verge of unraveling.

Her father sat back down at his desk, his pale eyes directed at her forehead. Green eyes. Green like Melony's. Aurelia's stomach turned. For years she had believed the supposed lack of blood ties between her and Melony was irrelevant. But blood had made all the difference—to her sister.

And who else had Aurelia misunderstood? "My mother," she said, the strange calm in her voice belying the turmoil in her chest. "Why did she leave? Was it because of your relationship with Elise?"

"That was her excuse, yes."

"You told me she abandoned us." That was all he had told her, and she had hated her mother. She had blamed her mother for her father's grief, for his need to remarry, for his choice of Elise as his wife. Because her mother was the one who had left.

But her father had left first. "She did abandon us," the king said. "She found out about Elise and Melony shortly after your brother's funeral. Your mother was already insane with grief. She blamed me for James's death, and threatened to tell the populace the truth about the accident if I didn't let her leave. She wanted to take you as well but came to her senses long enough to realize she could not discard your life as easily as her own.

"Your mother never learned to bend for politics," he continued with a frown. "I am afraid you inherited that trait from her. Perhaps it is my fault. I allowed you too much liberty."

Aurelia opened her mouth to protest, but he overrode her. "That is going to change." He straightened. "You will marry Edward of Anthone. I spoke with him this morning, and he is prepared to forgive your picnic escapade. The golden colt is yours. The tribes gave it to Edward as a gift for the future queen of Anthone."

Queen of Anthone. Bile rose in Aurelia's throat. "*I* am what he wanted from you?" she asked.

He nodded. "The kingdom of Anthone lies between Tyralt and your second cousin's kingdom of Montaine. With you as queen, our family will control the entire southern edge of the coast. If you have a child, one day both Anthone and Tyralt will be in his or her hands. I had hoped to barter for succession of the Anthonian throne even if you do not produce an heir. But the strife with your sister forces my hand. You are no longer safe in the palace. I have no choice but to let you go now."

Choice. He dared speak to her about choice.

"You could disown Melony," she said.

The king shook his head, and Aurelia thought she saw sorrow darken his face. "Melony was wrong, but she is still my daughter, Aurelia."

"She should be arrested."

His expression hardened. "Don't be naive. This family cannot afford another scandal."

No, you *cannot afford another scandal.* She saw now that it had not been grief that had kept him locked away the year after her brother's funeral and her mother's departure. It had been fear. Fear of scandal. Fear of what people would say.

For the first time, she saw her father as he really was, a weak man. His support of the investigation had been a charade. He had deliberately hidden the facts that would have allowed Robert to solve the case, and now he would not even consider arresting the instigator.

Instead he would marry his elder daughter to a man three times her age. The memory of Edward's index finger sliding along her chin made her shudder.

She wanted to pound on the desk and argue. She wanted to reason with her father. She wanted to dismantle his tilted, stained, self-centered version of reality. But nothing could be more powerful than the events played out on the racecourse that morning before his very eyes.

She stood up.

"Aurelia."

She walked out.

"You have not been dismissed."

The door clicked on her childhood.

Aurelia climbed the stairs to Henry's rooms, her thoughts running wild. *Betrayal*—the feeling stormed her defenses. Her father had betrayed her by refusing to punish her sister. Her sister had tried to kill her. And the queen? Had Elise known about Melony's plan? What did it matter when the king would do nothing to punish Elise either?

Somehow Aurelia felt that the queen would not have tolerated three failed attempts, much less four. No, Elise had never accepted failure.

And Melony had failed.

As had Aurelia. Failed at pleasing her father. Failed at pleasing the populace, for how could she become queen if she refused to marry the man of her father's choice? All the schooling, all the training, all the time spent trying to prove her worth had come to naught.

Yet somehow, it did not matter.

Courage. Aurelia knocked on the door.

Nothing.

Please, please be here. She knocked again, paused, listened.

Again nothing.

He just might not be answering. After all, the rooms did not belong to him. He might assume anyone coming to the door must be there for his uncle.

"Robert?" she called, knocking again. Something squeaked, and she held her breath.

Then nothing.

Maybe he did not want to talk to anyone. Maybe he was refusing to answer the door because he was angry. He deserved to be angry.

"Robert, it's me! Open the door." She pounded it with the flat of her hand.

Absolutely nothing.

Gone. Unable to accept the silence, she reached for the latch in frustration and pressed the lever, hard. It slid down. She released her grip and the door glided open.

Emptiness. She moved forward, peering into Uncle Henry's parlor. No bags, no mess, nothing that indicated someone might be packing for a journey.

Or that someone in the family had died.

She continued forward, heading for Chris's room. Robert had been staying there. If he had already left, his things would be gone. She opened the door, and pulled back in shock.

A body sprawled across the bed. Strands of blond hair sprayed over the pillow. Rumpled skirts and petticoats hitched up around torn stockings. Pale elbows splayed wide on quilt rings. Melony.

Aurelia stared, speechless. Even as a child, her sister had always arrived in style: face clean, hair brushed, dress spotless. Never had Aurelia seen Melony cast off her shoes at the foot of the bed as they were now, never out of control, never without manners, never anything less than perfect.

What was Melony doing here? In the room in which Robert had been staying?

"Where is he?" Aurelia asked, the back of her mind wondering how she could remain composed in the face of her sister's ultimate betrayal. But this was not the sister Aurelia had thought she knew, not the person she had comforted, confided in, and loved. Melony had incinerated those bonds and defined herself as a stranger.

The crumpled figure moved, palms digging into the covers, pushing up elbows and shoulders. A feral set of eyes peered out from behind the yellow net of loose strands. "Where is he?" Hollow words echoed back at her. "He's dead."

Chris, Aurelia realized. Her sister had come here because of Chris, not Robert. Despite what Robert had said about Chris's feelings for her sister, Aurelia had never imagined Melony would reciprocate. Not her sister. Not the one who dangled young men from her fingertips like string and twisted them around one another in an unending game of cat's cradle.

"Not Chris, Robert. Where is Robert?"

"Robert?" Melony's voice vibrated. "Our father let him go. He's gone."

Aurelia wanted to doubt the final words, but a glance around the room confirmed their truth. Nothing remained to indicate the room had even been lived in. The walls, the floor, the wardrobe—all stood bare. No swords, no clothes, no saddlebags. She moved to the door and swung it forward. No buckskin jacket.

"He's gone!" Melony's voice rose in hysteria. "He should be chained to a dungeon wall and left to starve until he's dead, like Chris. Dead!"

Aurelia backed away. "Where are Chris's things?"

"Father had them burned."

Why? Aurelia wanted to ask. Why would her father do that to Henry? But the answer came to her before she worded the question. The king would tell the public Chris was to blame for the assassination plot, for the unexplained events at the palace over the past four months, for the dead jockey on the racecourse that morning. Chris would be Father's scapegoat.

"It's your fault, you and your righteous act," Melony hissed. She brushed the hair off her face and sat up on her knees. "You don't really think you'll become queen of Tyralt, do you? Father is never going to put the throne in your hands. Mother says Edward can't have children. If he was going to have an heir, he'd already have one, and you aren't clever enough to have a child without him. You aren't even bright enough to keep your real feelings out of court."

The conversation with Melony outside Elise's dressing room suddenly made sense. "You were talking about your relationship with Chris," Aurelia accused, "when you said Father would never accept a suitor without a title."

Melony flung the crumpled pillow at her sister. "Now it doesn't matter, does it?!" she screamed. "You've destroyed everything. I hope Edward strangles you in your marriage bed."

"I'm not going to marry King Edward."

A bitter laugh ripped through the room. "Yes, you are. Father hasn't told you yet?"

"Yes, he told me." A strange calm settled into Aurelia's chest. She knew now that the only way to escape this insanity was to relinquish her political power. Let her father and sister suffer its dubious rewards. "But I'm not going to Anthone. I'm not staying here either. I'm leaving."

Chapter Fifteen
IN THE GARDEN

THE BRIDLE SLIPPED FROM ROBERT'S LEFT HAND. HE reached out instinctively with his right to catch the sliding leather, but the pain in his injured shoulder surprised him. And the bridle dropped unchecked to the stable floor.

He buried his head in Horizon's mane. He must leave. There was no question. The king had commanded it, and it was Robert's duty to obey.

Obedience, is that what you call it? The steady rise and fall of the stallion's belly did little to stave off Robert's scolding conscience. He should not leave without speaking to his uncle.

Perhaps Uncle Henry had known all along. Perhaps he also had been involved in the assassination plot. Robert had missed so many things, why not that as well? But Chris had said it was his father's idea to send for Brian Vantauge. Uncle Henry had written the letter. He had chosen to ask for help.

How could Robert explain what had happened? How could he ask forgiveness for having killed the son of a man he loved and respected? Robert knew he was too weak to do it.

Bending down, he lifted the bridle from the floor.

"I tell you, lad, you never cease to surprise me!" A mammoth black hand clapped down on Robert's good shoulder. The bridle went tumbling into a hay bale as Drew's familiar face grinned down at him. "I'm serious, lad," Drew said. "I consider myself a strong judge of character. It's a gift, you might say, the ability to see beyond the surface of most folks. But you, you show up at a horse fair, feed me a story, and ask me a simple question. When Her Highness arrived, I knew I was dealing with more than a lad interested in horses; but no matter how many times I revise my view of you, you keep surprising me."

Robert retrieved the bridle again, picking off strands of straw. "What do you mean?" he asked, struggling to adapt his senses to the older man's jovial energy.

"I mean I keep underrating you. I figured you for a friend of Aurelia's, harboring an infatuation, maybe, but nothing serious. Next thing I hear, you've asked permission to escort her on an outing, asked in the presence of the entire court no less. Lad," he said, shaking his head in disbelief, "I'd have paid gold coin to see that much gumption."

Robert dropped his head. The episode felt like a lifetime ago. "It wasn't what it seemed."

"That's my point." Drew pounded him on the back. "Then today, the streets are full of gossip: 'bout how the princess was found almost dead on the racecourse and you retaliated by killing one of the best fencers at the palace."

Robert shuddered and turned back to his horse. He could not bear the thought of having his actions heralded.

His companion did not take the hint; "I came up to hear the truth for myself; and not only are the rumors confirmed, but I also hear the same princess is embarking on an expedition of the kingdom. Mind you, the departure time for this grand tour is not a year from now, not a month, not even a week, but first thing tomorrow morning. Explain to me, lad, how Aurelia could have received permission for such a trip?"

Again the bridle fell to the ground. "It's not possible," Robert said, more to himself than to the man beside him. Not unless she had no choice. Not unless she, like Robert, had been ordered to leave. He clapped Drew's arm in apology for being rude and walked past the horseman back toward the palace.

Futility washed over Robert. He had failed. At everything. Beginning with that first night here. Aurelia had almost been poisoned at her sister's coming-out party, and he had never thought to connect the two events. Without his presence, she never would have been in danger on Carnival night because

Chris would never have seen her disguise. And she certainly would never have been alone in the arena this morning without his urging.

He should have known. Should have known he was in over his head when she had surprised him in Drew's tent, when she found out he was keeping something from her, when she had run away from him in the city. His father had been right. Robert had no business acting as royal spy. He had allowed his heart to make the decisions and let his feelings for Aurelia impair his judgment. He needed to apologize.

As if in answer to his thoughts, Uncle Henry intercepted him. The older man's fingers closed around Robert's upper left arm with surprising strength and led him across the courtyard, then around the outside of the west wing, where a vast lawn stretched out in terraces. Gray rectangular ponds ran through the center into the distance, and sculpted bushes lined the waterway. Even the plants in this place were manipulated by others.

Uncle Henry led his nephew past the main gardens into a walled alcove tucked between the back of the west wing and the older section of the palace. A small fountain trickled in a corner, and young trees and bushes lined the outskirts, their shades of green broken now and again by yellow flower buds. Robert sat down on the smooth stone ring surrounding the fountain and waited for his uncle's fury.

But the man whose son had died just stood staring at the

foliage as a breeze prickled the thin grasses and shuddery leaves. Memories hounded the quiet, memories of Chris: building towers of scrap wood in the carpentry shed, molding palaces of sand along the river's edge, making fun of fencing instructors in the practice yard.

Uncle Henry finally spoke, resignation lining his face. "Your father is a brave man." Robert started to stand, but his uncle waved him down. "He asked me to come with him when he left. I should have agreed, but I was too taken up with position and stability. It is ironic, I suppose, that his son has returned to show me the flimsiness of that stability."

Robert found his voice. "I am so sorry, Uncle Henry. I know nothing can atone for what I've done."

"I allowed you to take on the case. If there is guilt to be had, I must swallow as much as you." Henry looked down at him. "I cannot have you at the funeral, lad. Still, I do not blame you." A shaky hand rested on Robert's shoulder. For a moment the older man's eyes shone down too brightly. "You take after your father."

The words flowed like water into Robert's mind, cleansing the blood and the darkness. Not that the pain would ever go away. Or the loss.

Uncle Henry turned away, his shoulders more curved and his back more bent than they had been that morning. But there was strength in that body, in that mind. Strength beyond the physical.

"You could come with me now," Robert burst out. "I'm sure my father would welcome you."

The gray head shook. "I've served this ruler most of my life." There was a pause. "And I intend to live to serve a better one."

Henry? Aurelia slowed in her mad search of the palace grounds. Robert's uncle sat slouched on a low stoop, sunlight shining on his head as he stared blindly across the practice-yard sand. Her first reaction was to change direction, to allow space for his grief. An attempt to comfort him with her presence would do little but remind him of why his son had died. She turned to go...

Then stopped, remembering Chris's barren bedroom. How much did Henry know about what had happened today? Perhaps her father had told his adviser the truth. Henry had known about the assassination plot. He had known about Edward's desire to marry her. She suspected he knew Melony's true parentage as well. But she should speak to him, make certain he knew his son was not the sole culprit.

Slowly, she made her way to the older man's shoulder, allowing her feet to shuffle a bit on the marble path so as not to startle him. "Chris did it for Melony," she said, a sharp pain shooting through her chest as she spoke the names. "He was not in control of the plot. She was."

The older man waved a hand to quiet her. "I know," he said, then lapsed into silence.

She stood for a minute, uncertain what else to say to offer comfort; but as the seconds ticked by, her thoughts returned to her search for Robert. She had found Horizon in the stables and the filled saddlebags in the stall corner but had had no success tracking down the stallion's owner. She must find him, could not allow him to drift out of her life. "Have ... have you seen your nephew?" she asked softly, not wanting to injure Henry further but desperate enough to risk it.

A furrow creased his forehead as he looked at her. For a moment she thought he might burst out in anger as her sister had done. But his words, when they came, were resigned, not angry. "Robert was in the walled garden behind the east wing when I saw him last."

Her pulse quickened. She had not expected a real answer. "Thank you," she breathed, and turned to follow his directions.

A palm clasped her hand, holding her in check. "I had not meant to raise hopes, Your Highness," he said. "I saw my nephew there in the early afternoon. It has been several hours."

Her lips murmured that she understood, but her feet moved on at a hurried pace, gathering speed as she swept around the back of the palace. *The gardens;* she had looked there, but only on the main lawn, not in the walled alcove. She told herself not to expect him there. Not to hope.

The sun hit the horizon, light shimmering orange upon the leaves as she stepped into the garden. Her eyes found Robert. *He was there.* On the stone ring beside the fountain, one foot propped in front of him, shoulders curved, head facing away toward the tangled hedges. He did not see her.

How long had he been sitting there like this? Going over the events of the morning. Drowning in the horrors of this day.

Nerves roiled within her stomach. Could she tell him what she must—in the right way? In a way that would ease the pain? Not erase it. No words, no actions, could eliminate the truth of that mangled body crumpled in the soil, the hatred brimming from her sister's face, the empty husk of her father's weakness. And no words could bring back Chris.

"It isn't your fault." She let her voice ring in the stillness.

Robert lifted his head without turning to face her. "I killed my own cousin."

"I know," she said, her gaze falling to his wounded shoulder. "I'm sorry."

Still, he did not turn around. Perhaps he was angry with her for not standing up to her father. She remembered her alarm at Robert's dismissal. But at the time it was only one more nightmarish event in a morning of revelations. She had been reeling from the discovery of her sister's malice and her father's deceit. And she had failed to speak up on Robert's behalf.

"My father wasn't strong enough to make the right decision," she tried to explain. "I should have known he wouldn't be, but I didn't."

"He was right," Robert said.

"No, he wasn't." She could not allow him to believe that.

"He was right about me placing you in danger. This morning I thought I understood everything: the plan, the plot, my feelings for you . . ." Robert trailed off. "Then when I saw you fall on the racecourse and I thought you were dead . . ." There was a long pause. "I don't ever want to feel that way again, Aurelia."

Her heart thundered, and she took a step closer.

Still he did not turn. "And now you've been exiled." Robert lifted a hand through his dark hair. "I put your life at risk for nothing."

She stared at him, confused. Why would he feel guilt for her exile? But that was Robert, trying to shoulder responsibility for a task neither her father nor his had dared take on. "No," she replied. "I chose to leave." She struggled to put her revelation into words. "My father wants me to marry Edward of Anthone, and that is an exile I cannot accept. I'm done living my life in the confines of others' dreams, done waiting to live my own. I am going on an expedition of Tyralt." She stepped closer.

Robert lowered his hand, dropping it to the stone surface. His back rose and fell. "What about your father?"

"My father is not brave enough to stop me. He is terrified of scandal." Bitterness slipped out with her words. "No doubt he'll announce that I've relinquished my right to the throne and name Melony in my place, but he will also provide me with the supplies and an armed escort for my expedition because he won't want me to tell the populace what really happened today. I am going to travel every inch of the kingdom if I wish. No one will dictate where I go or whom I see." Determination sprouted in Aurelia's chest. "Let Melony use her powers of persuasion to avoid marrying Edward. I will meet the people of this kingdom, *my* kingdom, whether or not I wear a crown."

"A leader is not decided by a crown," Robert said, "but by the people who believe in and follow that leader."

She had no response for that. Her mind was already racing ahead to what she needed to say next. Her hands clenched with the fear of laying bare her heart.

"You're leaving in the morning?" he asked in a hollow voice.

"Yes... but I have a problem." She was now quite close to Robert, so close she could hear his unsteady breathing. Fear of rejection flared in her chest. Perhaps he would prefer a life on the frontier, without politics and her royal shadow. *But that night on the bridge,* her heart argued, *he said he wanted to see the corners of the world.* She pushed aside the fear and leaped. "I need an expedition guide."

The terror of silence met her statement.

But now she had begun, she must finish. "A guide I can trust." Her words came out slow and deliberate. "Someone who knows the land and does not mind traveling and meeting new people."

He inhaled sharply.

"You," she said, "are the only person I can trust."

He turned now and faced her, his blue eyes wide with the

possibility she presented. That gaze. There was power in that gaze, something that drew her in and held her. But it was not constricting. It did not push down on her from above. It simply was. And her heart told her it was a good place to be.

"Aurelia." His voice wavered.

"Please, Robert," she whispered. "I need you at my side." She stretched out a hand and ran it along the edge of his face. There were traces of tearstains there and hurt and anger, but they were all old, covered now by a different emotion. "Will you guide my expedition?"

Fingertips brushed like feathers across her cheek, and a thread wound up within her at his touch. "I would be honored," he said.

Epilogue

HORIZON DID NOT SEEM TO CARE FOR THE CHAOS IN
the courtyard prior to departure. He snorted and stamped his
hooves, powdered dust billowing up in a fresh wave.

Aurelia felt the dust enter her lungs. She coughed and pulled
away from Robert's side. "Can't you convince him to stop?" she
said, struggling to see her expedition guide through the brown
fog.

"He would relax if everyone else would," Robert argued.

Half a dozen guards milled behind them, clapping friends
on the back and shouting good-byes. Family members bearing
last-minute keepsakes rushed up to the guards. Horses shuffled,
sensing the excitement in the air. Servants swarmed out of
the palace, shuttling bundles to wagons and mounts, and men
shouted from the tops of the wagons that they had no more

room; but the bundles kept coming, and the men kept rearranging and piling on things.

"This is ridiculous," Robert complained. "Each person should bring enough for him or herself, and that's it. We can restock later if necessary. The rest of the kingdom is not entirely uncivilized."

Drew chuckled. "Lad, you'd best get used to it. A royal expedition is twenty percent loading and unloading."

Robert groaned. "Not if I have anything to say about it." He handed the horseman Horizon's reins and swung down to the ground.

"Hey!" Drew protested. "Where are you going? You're not leaving me with this dust maker."

"I'm doing what needs to be done to stop Horizon from making dust." Robert marched off toward the wagons.

Drew arched an eyebrow at Aurelia. "Do you think he'll return to us in one piece?"

"Not if the kitchen maids get hold of him." She laughed and patted Bianca, then looked up to see Drew disappear in another brown cloud.

"I wish you were coming the entire journey with us," she said.

"Ha! I'm starting to wonder if I'll even make it to the next town. Don't be surprised if you wake up tomorrow morning and find I've lit out."

"No," she protested. "You promised to stay with us at least a week."

"I am not spending a week watching over this horse."